**Diana picked up the knife,
said, "Now,"
and cut into the Viscount Alma's flesh.**

There was a muffled oath through the leather that the lord had clenched between his teeth, and Diana worked quickly to remove the arrow within minutes. When she had dropped it to the floor, she staunched the copious flow of blood with the cloths provided and applied the astringent. Turning to her brother George with a smile she said, "That is all you will need me for; I trust you can wrap it." Without another word she picked up the arrow and her knife and left the room.

"Efficient little wench," Alma muttered as he took the leather from his mouth.

"She's very handy to have around. You should be grateful to her," George commented dryly.

"I should have been more grateful if she had not shot me in the first place."

"To be sure," her brother replied, "but the accident was as much your fault as hers, so I beg you will forget it."

The wounded man grinned crookedly and remarked, "Since I shall not be able to sit comfortably for some time, I doubt I shall be able to forget it. However, though I can endeavor to hold no hard feelings, I cannot imagine myself married to a woman who could shoot me anytime it pleased her."

"Never mind," George replied blandly. "It was never more than a thought."

Also by Laura Matthews

The Seventh Suitor

Published by
WARNER BOOKS

Your Warner Library of Regency Romance

The Aim of a Lady

Laura Matthews

WARNER BOOKS

A Warner Communications Company

WARNER BOOKS EDITION

Copyright © 1980 by Elizabeth Rotter
All rights reserved.

ISBN: 0-446-94341-X

Cover art by Walter Popp

Warner Books, Inc., 75 Rockefeller Plaza, New York, N.Y. 10019

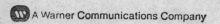 A Warner Communications Company

Printed in the United States of America

First Printing: June, 1980

10 9 8 7 6 5 4 3 2 1

For Matt and Laura,
with love.

chapter one

"But, George, I did not *mean* to shoot him," Diana protested, as she attempted to match her brother's lengthy strides. "I was merely practicing, as I do every day, and Rogue bounced on me and made me miss the target." Diana was forced to stop speaking for a moment in order to catch her breathe and run a few steps to regain her brother's side. "Really, it was quite foolish of him to gallop right behind my target. He must have seen it!"

George Savile gave an exasperated shrug. "You must have heard his horse, Diana."

"I did hear a horse, yes; but everyone around here knows where I practice and they always look to see if I am out. I *am* sorry," she said penitently.

"I hope you told him so," her brother replied mildly.

"Well, I did, but he will not look at me. I am sure I have never seen him before. He simply roared at me to bring him some help, and so I came for you immediately." They were past the stables now and headed toward the Home Wood where Diana's archery target stood out glaringly red and white in the spring sunlight.

"Oh, my God," her brother sighed. His eyes had lit now on the prostrate form beyond the target, and the dappled stallion nudging its fallen rider. "I have had the worst feeling since you burst into the library that it would be Ellis, and it is."

"I cannot see how you can tell," Diana objected. "He is still lying there turned away. He said the arrow was too deep for him to pull out."

"No doubt," George replied dampeningly. "The stallion is well known to me, Diana. Dear God, you did not bother to tell me where you hit him!"

For the first time since she had raced for her brother Diana colored fiercely. "Well, George, it is why I did not try to take care of the matter myself," she admitted.

7

Ellis James Thomas Robbins, Eighth Viscount Alma, had received Diana's missent arrow in his right buttock. He had been startled when this occurred, and it had taken him a moment to realize what had happened and, dumbfounded, to rein in his horse. He had dismounted, to Diana's amazement, with a casualness and aplomb hardly creditable under the circumstances. Without a glance at her he had attempted to remove the offending items, but when he was unsuccessful his knees seemed to buckle and he crumpled before her eyes. She had dashed to his aid, stricken with guilt, but when he heard her approach he said firmly, "Do not touch me. What the devil do you think you're doing, shooting arrows at people?" Diana understood, even with his face turned away, that he was beginning to lose his temper, and she stuttered an apology. She assumed it was the pain which made him roar at her to get him some help.

Diana now slowed her steps as her brother approached the wounded man. "Have a problem, old man?" George asked calmly.

"Devil take you, George! Send the girl away and take this confounded thing out of me."

George placed a tentative hand on the shaft of the arrow and cautiously attempted to pull it. The feel of its penetration made him whistle. "Diana has outdone herself," he murmured.

"Your sister, I doubt not," his friend gasped as a wave of pain swept over him.

"Yes. I shall introduce you sometime, but now I think I had best get you to the Park. Can you walk if I support you?"

"I suppose so. Don't leave Crusader here, though. I tell you, George, if she had hit the horse I would have choked her with my own two hands."

"I would not have been pleased," George returned gently. "I am fond of her." He raised his voice to call to his sister, who still maintained a wary distance. "Take his horse to the stables, Diana, if you please."

Lord Alma protested faintly, "She is not to ride him, damnit. Make her lead him."

8

"Lead him, please," George amended his instructions as his sister approached the animal.

Diana cast a derogatory glance at the injured man, now being helped to his feet, but nodded her acceptance. She spoke to the horse soothingly and grasped his reins. Without a backward glance she walked off across the field toward the stables.

"You really should know better than to ride behind an archery target, Ellis, especially when you can see that someone is using it."

"I shall remember in future."

The two men proceeded slowly to the house beyond the stables. George took his friend to the room which had been prepared for his arrival and gave instructions to send for the surgeon apothecary in the village.

"You cannot expect me to lie here with this *thing* in me until some country dolt arrives to remove it," Lord Alma protested, his irritation surfacing anew.

"He will do a better job of it than I could. I dare say Diana could do it, but I doubt you would let her."

"Sometimes I am grateful for your profound understanding," his friend muttered into the pillow. The black hair curled damply on his brow and George shortly provided him with a cloth to wipe his perspiring forehead. Suddenly Lord Alma gave a burst of laughter and turned his head to meet George's eyes. "I have never felt so ridiculous in my life, but I must admit that I was careless. I had thought to take a shortcut to your stables and was more intent on getting one last gallop out of Crusader than on what your sister was doing."

"It is rare for her to miss the target; she says the dog jumped on her."

"There *was* a dog. I heard one bark. Does she shoot people often?"

"Not to my knowledge, but I am not often here. I would doubt it, though, as she is an excellent shot."

"I am gratified to hear it. I do not think I should like to marry her, though, George," his friend said somewhat apologetically.

"Never mind. It was never more than a thought,"

George replied blandly. "Diana is disgustingly happy with her life just as it is. I doubt even you could entice her away from it."

"It's not that she's not an attractive female," Lord Alma admitted generously. "The one glimpse I got of her before the arrow hit me was not the least disturbing, I promise you. But I cannot imagine myself married to a woman who could shoot me anytime it pleased her, rather as though it were an accident."

"I understand perfectly, Ellis. We need not discuss the matter further. Very unfortunate you should have met her under such circumstances, but I cannot say I blame you a whit." George deposited himself carefully on the edge of the bed and tentatively touched the shaft of the arrow again. "I can try to take it out, if you wish."

"You would butcher me," his friend replied amiably. "I have seen you carve a ham, remember."

There was a scratching at the door and George's valet entered when bidden. "Mr. Thatcher is away from home and not expected back until very late, sir."

George nodded absently. "Do you think you could remove this arrow, Stephen?"

The valet paled at the thought but answered smoothly, "No, sir, I do not."

"I thought not. Whom in the household would you suggest?"

The valet once again eyed the location of the offending arrow. "I should not like to suggest the logical party."

"No, of course not. Would you get Lord Alma out of his boots and breeches, please?" George rose from the bed while the valet removed the boots. When he had disappeared to obtain a knife to cut the buckskins, George said, "I will ask around the house, Ellis. Someone is likely to feel capable of removing the arrow."

"Take your time," Ellis drawled, and swung his head around to meet his friend's eyes. "Who is the logical party?"

"Need you ask?"

"No, of course not. The goddess of archery herself, no doubt, with plenty of experience in removing the fruits of her labors," he sighed.

"Not that so much as that she assists the apothecary when he needs her, and she is sometimes called in when he cannot be reached."

"George," Lord Alma asked patiently, "why did you conceive of the idea of marrying off your sister to me? Did you think me in need of my own personal apothecary?"

"She has many interests; that is only one of them."

"I will not burden you with enlightening me on the others. Find someone to remove the arrow, George."

With a mocking smile George agreed and left his friend to meditate on his distressing situation. George himself unsuccessfully scoured the house for a potential surgeon, and then left for the stables. There he found his sister speaking with the head groom, who was admiring Crusader as he brushed the stallion.

Diana cast a look of enquiry at her brother, who shook his head sadly and said, "Mr. Thatcher is not available. Other than yourself, my dear, who here might be able to remove the arrow?"

His sister eyed the workers in the stables and suggested Jenkins, who brought his head up with such speed that he grazed it against the side of the loose box. "Oh no, Miss. Never would I take a knife to a viscount. Not on your life, begging your pardon."

George thoughtfully considered the man. "You would not find it difficult, Jenkins. If he were a horse, it would not bother you at all."

"I have never shot a horse," Diana declared indignantly.

"You never shot a man before either, my dear. The arrow must be removed. What do you say, Jenkins?"

"I couldn't do it, sir," the man protested passionately.

"Never mind. Diana, come with me."

Diana followed her brother from the stables into the late afternoon sunlight. "Would it embarrass him so much for me to do it? she asked.

"Yes."

"Did you tell him that I have worked with Mr. Thatcher?"

"Yes."

"Then he is foolish. He cannot wish to lie around with an arrow in him all day."

"No, he has instructed me to find someone to remove it."

"Then I shall, with no more to-do. Give him something to drink and a piece of leather to bite and I will be with you in a few minutes. Tell Mrs. Hobson to send hot water, clean cloths and basins. I will bring my knife and some astringent."

Her brother nodded skeptically and parted with her in the hall. When she arrived at Lord Alma's room some little time later, she tapped firmly on the door. George opened it himself but did not let her pass. "He will not have you do it."

"Are the supplies here?"

"Yes."

"Then let us get on with it."

"Diana, he will not let you do it."

"How is he to stop me?" she asked exasperatedly. "It will take but a few minutes, George, and you can simply hold him down."

There was a startled grunt from the direction of the bed. George continued to block his sister's passage but turned his head to meet his friend's astonished gaze. "I think I should let her complete her handiwork, Ellis. I cannot have you lying about with an arrow in you for the next few hours."

Alma gave a resigned shrug. "Very well." He made an attempt to partially cover his bare bottom with a sheet, but determinedly maintained a stoic calm in the face of the inevitable. Diana was allowed into the room and set a rather grim looking knife on the bedside stand beside the hot water and cloths sent up by Mrs. Hobson. "I am pleased that you have agreed, Lord Alma. You need not be concerned. It will not be the first time I have been called upon in an emergency."

George produced the brandy decanter and offered his friend a second glass, which Alma took with a steady hand and drained rapidly. Taking the arrow shaft in her hand, Diana determined the depth of penetration. "You will have to roll over on your side, my lord," she said gently.

Alma cast a hopeless glance at his friend and did as he was told, clutching the sheet to cover as much of himself as he could. When George offered him the bit of leather he had procured, Alma took it resignedly and put it between his teeth. Diana picked up the knife, said, "Now" and cut into his flesh. There was a muffled oath through the leather, and the hand grasping the sheet clenched into a fist which bunched the sheet about the arrow. Diana prised apart Alma's fingers and pushed the sheet gently out of the way. There was no further sound from her patient and she worked quickly to have the arrow out within minutes. When she had dropped it to the floor, she staunched the copious flow of blood with the cloths provided and applied the astringent. Turning to George with a smile she said, "That is all you will need me for. I trust you can wrap it yourself." Without another word she picked up the gory arrow and her knife, and left the room.

"Efficient little wench," Alma muttered as he took the leather from his mouth.

"She's very handy to have around. You should be grateful to her," George commented dryly.

"I should have been more grateful if she had not shot me in the first place."

"To be sure, but it was as much your fault as hers, so I beg you will forget it."

The wounded man gave a crooked grin and remarked, "Since I shall not be able to sit comfortably for some time, I doubt I shall be able to forget it. However, I can endeavor to hold no hard feelings." Alma obediently rolled over for George to finish wrapping the awkwardly placed injury. "How old is she?"

"Almost three-and-twenty."

"She did not seem the least bit embarrassed to see me naked," Alma said accusingly.

"You were a patient to her. She has cared for a vast array of sick people at the Park and in the village as well, when necessary."

"That duty is usually reserved for married women."

"Ellis, there is nothing unfeminine about Diana. On the other hand, there is nothing missish about her either. She is just not like other women. I have told you we will drop the idea of promoting a match between the two of you. Get some sleep and I will have dinner brought up to you later."

Since the two rapidly consumed glasses of brandy were already dulling the pain and making it difficult for Alma to concentrate on his friend's voice, he fell asleep immediately after George left. But he had dreams of being attacked by red Indians, with arrows sticking all about his body, and he woke in the dimming light of evening in a sweat.

chapter two

"I would like to know why you were using hunting arrows," George remarked to his sister when they were seated at their meal. He continued to dissect his sturgeon with enthusiasm but his gaze on her was quizzical.

"They have a different weight about them. It is all very well to be accurate with the target arrows, George, but it would be remiss of me to never achieve the same level of competence with a hunting arrow. They were the smallest we have. Did Lord Alma say something?" She raised her troubled hazel eyes from her plate to meet his.

"I am sure he has not the slightest idea of the difference and I did not find it necessary to enlighten him. But it will take some time for the wound to heal and it will leave quite a scar. I pray you will not use them again."

"Very well. It made little difference in my scoring in any case." They were silent for a while and then she asked, "Does he stay long?"

"I cannot be sure. He certainly won't be able to go anywhere soon."

"No, he will be most uncomfortable for some time. I *am* sorry, George."

"I know you are. It was unfortunate, but Ellis says he will try to harbor no ill will. How did Rogue get onto your range?"

"I had locked him in the stable, but Jenkins says one of the boys gave in to his piteous cries and released him to play with him. Of course, he took off after me immediately. It was just a series of misadventures," she sighed as she sipped her wine, her forehead puckered in a frown.

"No matter. The problem will be to keep Ellis entertained, since he will not be able to ride. Have you any suggestions?" His brown eyes lightly mocked her.

"I could teach him to shoot a bow and arrow," she offered mischievously.

"I doubt he would be interested."

"When he is bored enough he might change his mind," she replied seriously. "Oh he might like to fence with you or me. I seldom have anyone as an opponent with you away so often."

"I have not taken care of you as I ought," George admitted, "But since you do not wish to go to London . . ."

"Don't be absurd. I am not complaining of your absence. I would no more keep you here than allow you to carry me off to town. There is no sense in my going to London when I would only pine for the Park. I have my friends and my interests here, George, and you have yours elsewhere, though I know you love the Park as dearly as I do."

Her brother watched the dusk gathering outside the dining parlor window, softening the shapes of the trees until they blended with the sky. He was of average height, where Diana was very small, but they had the same brown hair. His countenance, with a straight nose and calm brown eyes, rarely varied from easy good humor. "I am thinking of marrying, Diana."

Her hazel eyes met his, unwavering and calm. "I have expected that you would some day. Do I know the lady?"

"No, for I only met her in town in the fall. I have not approached her as yet. She's Lord Franston's youngest, Alonna. Several things have come up which have kept me from town, so I have not seen her as often as I would have liked." George made an impatient gesture with his fork. "It may be that she will not have me, of course."

"Nonsense. Tell me about her." Diana indicated to the footman that she had finished her meal and sat back in her chair with an interested expression on her countenance. Her brown hair gleamed in the candlelight and her high cheekbones accentuated the delicacy of her features. She was a tiny woman, plainly dressed, but glowing with health from outdoor living.

George contemplated the glass of wine in his hand and attempted to describe Alonna. "She is taller than you, and a few years younger, with blond hair and blue eyes. Rather pretty, I think, but she would never be the season's beauty. She dances well and has the usual accomplishments." He shrugged helplessly. "Lord, I don't know how to describe her, Diana."

"Does she share your interests? Can you talk to her easily? Does she prefer life in the country or in town?"

He looked thoughtful for a moment, fingering a gold fob absently. "I think the reason I have considered marrying her is because I *can* talk to her. She doesn't want for sense. I have not visited her in Hampshire as yet, but she speaks of the country fondly. Yet she is at home in the city as well, though she is inexperienced in society. I think you will like her."

"I am sure I shall. But, George, you must remember what we decided long ago in the event of your marrying. I shall move into the Dower House so that you may have the Park to yourselves." There was no trace of sadness or anger in her voice or countenance.

"Hardly something we decided. *You* have always proclaimed that you would do so, and *I* have never seen the least need. Besides, everything is far from being settled."

"I see what it is," she taunted. "You wish for me to make a scene so that you may reconsider your decision and martyr yourself to your sister!"

His brown eyes lit with appreciative mockery. "What it is, Diana, is that I fear I am too old to marry such a child. She is very trusting and open, and I am not sure that I should not offer for someone a little more . . . experienced. Alonna is not just out of the schoolroom, you understand. She must be close on twenty. Lady Franston died a year ago and had been ill for some time before that, so Alonna has only recently been brought to town."

"You are only five-and-thirty, George. Would you like for me to come to town with you to meet her?"

"Heaven forbid! Though I had thought of it," he said sheepishly, "and I had intended to leave for town with Ellis in a few days." He frowned uncertainly. "I do not like to leave him here alone with you, Diana, but I have begun to feel rather . . . anxious to speak with Alonna."

"Are there others paying court to her?" she asked curiously.

"Yes, and I do not like to leave her in doubt of my intentions any longer than is strictly necessary."

"Lord Alma will not like it, but I fear you must go. I shall keep him entertained until he's ready to depart." She rose to leave him and placed a hand affectionately on his arm. "I wish you well, George."

"Thank you. I would stay a few days, but I had a letter today from Cranmer . . . well, I shall speak with Ellis."

Lord Alma was aghast. "You do not intend to leave me here with your sister? No, that's too much, George. Who will play propriety for her? Or do you intend to trap me into marrying her?" he asked bitterly, a hand creeping gingerly toward his aching bottom.

George gave a snort of laughter. "I assure you, Ellis, that my sister does not concern herself overmuch with such matters as propriety, but I will have Mrs. Lewis from the village come in to stay if it will calm your overwrought nerves. I really must go to town." His troubled frown was not ignored by his friend.

"Oh, never mind me. I'm wallowing in self-pity just now because you have not as yet had my dinner sent up," Alma reminded him with a grin.

George lifted a brow in query. "Someone must have come and found you asleep." He rang and gave instructions for his friend's meal. "I know it is rude of me to desert you, and I had no intention of doing so, but Cranmer's letter indicated that Lord Vallert is buzzing about Alonna rather seriously, and I should kick myself if I missed my chance."

"There will be other ladies," Alma retorted philosophically.

George shook his head slowly. "If so, I wonder that I have met no one in the last fifteen years that I considered marrying."

"Oh, go to London, you gudgeon," Alma said gruffly. "I shall manage very well here, I have no doubt. How long do you suppose it will be before I can ride?"

"Several weeks, I should think, before it's comfortable. Diana offered to teach you to shoot a bow and arrow."

"Has she no tact, either?" asked his exasperated friend.

"Enough, I should think. She fences, too."

Alma regarded him perplexedly. "Do you fence with her?"

"Yes, but not very often. She's a beginner and would not provide much sport for you, but she's eager to develop the skill."

"George, I thought you told me she was not unfeminine."

George smiled benignly down at him. "When you see her in her fencing outfit . . . well, forget it. Perhaps it is well that you will not." The invalid's meal arrived then, and there was some debate as to the easiest manner in which for him to eat it. Chagrined, he eventually did so while standing up.

George rang for a deck of cards and the two men played an awkward game of piquet after Alma finished his meal. The wounded man lay on his stomach on his bed, wrong way about, and the cards were placed on the counterpane. The inconvenience of his posture began to tell on Alma's nerves after a while and he pushed the cards away from him with annoyance.

"I think I had best return to Stillings tomorrow, George."

"I understand how you feel, old man," his friend agreed sympathetically, "but it really cannot be done—even in a carriage. Diana will keep you amused. And if you think of her as a younger brother you will not feel so blue-devilled. It was a mistake to bring you here," he sighed, "and I would not have done so, except that when it actually came to my considering marriage I thought perhaps Diana would be comfortably settled first. But she has had sufficient opportunities and I should have left well enough alone. She tells me she intends to move into the Dower House if I marry, and it does not appear to trouble her in the least. In fact, she seemed genuinely pleased that I had found someone I *wanted* to marry. You have no pressing engagements, have you?"

"No, nothing of moment." Alma drew his hand through his black hair absently. His black brows above intensely blue eyes were expressive of his emotions, and they were now drawn up in self-mockery. He ran a hand gently over his aching wound. "I am in some pain, George."

"Lord, why did you not say so?" George rose abruptly and gathered the cards together. "I shall have Diana bring you some laudanum right away."

"Has my man arrived with my clothing?"

"Yes, while you were asleep. Shall I send him to you?"

"Please. And do not bother your sister—my man can take care of me."

"As you wish. I shall speak with you before I leave in the morning. I regret the inconvenience to you, Ellis."

"I appreciate your understatement, Savile. I shall remember in future to accept any invitations to your home with great caution." His sardonic tone did not obscure the fact that his face was pinched with pain, and his host hastened to send for his valet.

When Rodgers arrived, George bid his friend sleep well and slipped out the door into the candle-lit hall. He felt restless and in need of company, so he asked where his sister might be found and joined her in the music room. She was seated at the harpsichord playing a haunting tune of the countryside. George seated himself comfortably on the upholstered settee and closed his eyes until she had finished the piece.

"Is something the matter, George?" Diana asked with concern.

"I cannot shake the feeling . . . no, nothing is wrong. Ellis is having some pain but his man has gone to him. I am leaving in the morning, Diana. I told Ellis I would have Mrs. Lewis come in while he is here for the sake of appearance. You will not mind?"

"No, she's a dear soul. Do not delay yourself; I will go to her in the morning. Come, sing with me a while."

Diana started to finger a more cheerful song and her brother joined his voice with hers. The strains of their music reached Alma in his bedchamber as he drifted into a restless sleep.

chapter three

"No, Papa, there can have been no mistake on Lord Vallert's part," Alonna Sanfield said angrily. Her blazing eyes lifted from the announcement in the *Herald*. "I realize he had your permission to pay his addresses to me, but I did *not* accept him. It is beyond anything for him to have sent an announcement to the *Herald*. You will have to have him retract it."

"Now, now, my dear. Let's not be hasty. He's a good young fellow—nice manners, pleasant spoken, plenty of the ready," he exhorted bluffly.

"I had thought him pleasant enough myself, Papa, until this!" Alonna jumped up from her chair in the breakfast parlor and paced restlessly about the room. "I will not be forced into marrying him just because he has been so rash as to place the announcement. How dare he!"

"You are not getting any younger, Alonna. It is time you were married. You could not do better than Vallert, I assure you," her red-faced parent blustered. "So he was a trifle premature; it only shows how eager he is."

"It shows how unprincipled he is," his daughter retorted coldly. "I have not been in town so long as to wear my welcome thin as an unmarried lady in society. My sisters each had sufficient time given them to make a match of their choice, and I hope that you do not intend to rush me into marriage now that Mama is dead."

Her father had the grace to flush, but a sly gleam entered his eye as he said, "I take it you are waiting for some other young man to come up to scratch, miss."

Alonna did not allow him to see that he had discomfited her. "I will not marry Lord Vallert after this fiasco, Papa, so you must have him retract the announcement of our engagement." She walked from the room with all the dignity she possessed.

It would destroy her, she thought. How could he

do such a thing? Lord Vallert had recently essayed a whirl-wind courtship of her; and she had tried desperately, in her inexperience, to keep him at arm's length. When he had called to offer for her he had been elegantly dressed and self-assured; her refusal had left him nonplussed. The handsome, aristocratic face had become blank and then flushed. "You cannot understand, Miss Sanfield. I wish for you to be my wife."

Alonna had not meant to laugh, and could have throttled herself for having done so, but he had looked too ridiculous. "I assure you I do understand, Lord Vallert, and I am honored by your offer. Though our acquaintance has not been of long duration, I do not believe we would suit."

His eyes had grown furious at her laugh, which he considered the ultimate in insults. "We should become better acquainted during our engagement," he said stiffly.

"That is putting the cart before the horse," she answered sensibly, with an attempt at a conciliating smile.

"Your father has given his permission."

"That is hardly enough to ensure a successful marriage," Alonna said quietly. "In this case it means merely that he would not forbid me to marry you, not that I must. Please understand, Lord Vallert, that I hold you in esteem and do not wish to offend you, but I cannot marry you."

"We shall see," he had muttered as he bowed and left the room.

Alonna had not expected any repercussions from this proposal. It had taken place two days previously and she had not seen Lord Vallert in the meantime. His place-ment of the announcement had been done in a fit of pique, she imagined, but it would nonetheless cause her great embarrassment. An immediate retraction was ob-ligatory, and even that would cause a great deal of talk in London. When a footman came to announce callers, she had them denied. The headache which she used as an excuse was fast becoming a reality.

There had been no hesitation in refusing Lord Val-lert. It was not that she really supposed that she had made any impression on George Savile, though that was her fondest wish. He was much older than she, some fifteen years, but she had enjoyed his company so much that she found Lord Vallert and his contemporaries dull in comparison. Nevertheless, she knew she must appear inexperienced and unsophisticated to Savile, who had spent the greater part of his adult years in London and at the country seats of his numerous aristocratic friends. She had not seen him so very many times, at that, though she treasured each encounter and replayed it in her mind often enough. Now what would he think of her when her engagement was announced one day and withdrawn the next.

George took leave of his sister and friend in the morning, which was the day the announcement of Alonna's betrothal appeared in London. He continued to feel the sense of urgency which had been generated by his friend's letter and covered the sixty miles to the capital in less than seven hours.

Behind him he left a sister determined to entertain his friend to the best of her ability, since she still suffered a certain amount of guilt in relation to the incident, and a friend determined to avoid any further contact with his sister, since she had provided him with sufficient pain and embarrassment to last his dignified self a lifetime. It was not a propitious beginning.

When Alma responded to a light tap on his door Diana stood in the doorway and bid him good morning. "I hope you are not still in pain, my lord," she said when she met his unwelcoming scowl. "I can send for Mr. Thatcher if you wish."

"That will not be necessary, as my man assures me the wound is healing well enough," he replied stiffly.

"I'm glad to hear it. Do you plan to stay in bed today?" she asked curiously.

"I had not decided as yet."

"If you should like to get up now, I shall wait for you and you can walk with me to Linton to speak with Mrs. Lewis. George would like her to stay while you are here," she explained, a mischievous smile playing about her lips. "Are you so dangerous?"

He choked quietly where he lay on his stomach in

the fourposter. "Not in the least, Miss Savile, and especially when I am wounded."

"Then come. It will do you more good to walk with me than to lie about your bed. If you are tired later, I will read to you."

Alma cast her a malignant glance and said stonily, "I am quite able to read, Miss Savile."

"Excellent, Lord Alma. I'll send your man to help you and will wait for you in the music room." Before he had time to protest she softly closed the door.

He entered the music room nearly a half hour later to hear her play the concluding notes of a song which she hummed in accompaniment of herself. She looked up with a smile and he hestitantly returned it. "It does feel better to be up," he admitted grudgingly. "I fell asleep while you and George were singing last night."

"How flattering! Perhaps you will sing with me this evening."

"Perhaps."

"Lord Alma," Diana said, as she rose from her seat at the harpsichord and came around to him, "was George wrong when he told me you would not hold a grudge for the accident?"

"No, of course not. It was as much my fault as yours."

"Then you are still upset that I took out the arrow," she surmised. "You should not be. We all find ourselves in undignified positions at times and it is better to laugh at them than to suffer from them. I assure you, it did not damage your consequence in my eyes or George's, so you must be the only one to regard it so." She extended her hand to him, her eyes smiling kindly.

Alma gave a rueful grin and shook her hand. "As you say, Miss Savile. Let us forget it."

Diana nodded. "I think you will like Linton. The River Granta flows by and then through the Park, and there are the most fascinating old buildings—a timbered inn, a gabled house with raised plaster work and thatched cottages. The Guildhall and the church are both worthy, too." She continued to enlighten him concerning local history as they passed into the park and through an ancient

25

clapper stile with bars that fell at a touch to let them pass over and then slipped back again. Diana led him first to the thatched cottage where Mrs. Lewis lived and disappeared inside when he chose to walk about alone.

Mrs. Lewis, the widow of a naval officer, welcomed the young woman warmly and offered her a cup of tea. The widow had resided in Linton for most all the years of Diana's life and was a fixture in the village. She was short and round, with apple-bright cheeks only slightly wrinkled by age.

"Such a lovely day, Miss Diana, and I hear your brother has returned to the Park," she chirped happily as she prepared the tea for them.

"Been and gone," Diana laughed. "He hastened to London this morning."

"But he had only just arrived! I know you were looking forward to seeing him."

"Yes, but his business was urgent. He had invited a friend to stay and I have come to ask if you will join me at the Park for a few weeks, Mrs. Lewis. Lord Alma has been injured and George thought it would be best if you could come to stay, since his lordship cannot very well leave."

"Is that he?" Mrs. Lewis asked as she watched a stranger stroll down the street. "He does not appear to be ill."

"No, he is feeling well enough, but the injury necessitates his remaining. He cannot ride or drive for a while."

"I see," her companion said, though she obviously did not. "Well, Miss Diana, there is nothing I would enjoy more than to stay with you. When shall I come?"

"I will send the carriage for you and your luggage after luncheon, if you can be ready by then."

The two women sat for a while and drank their tea, discussing the village and its recent happenings, before Diana excused herself to join Alma. "We are saved," she grinned at him. "Mrs. Lewis can come."

"I am grateful," he sighed comically. As he walked along beside her, a bit of a limp appeared when he tired, though he was enjoying the warm sunshine.

"Let me show you the church," she offered when she noted his limp. It was frustrating that he could not sit down to rest but he could lean against the arches resting on their Norman pillars. He hesitated to do so, determined not to show his weakness, but followed her lead when she rested against the cold stone. She pointed out the brass portrait of Nicholas Paris ("when we were children we called him Nick") done in 1427, in armor with a lion and a sword. There was also the curious last-century family group in marble depicting a man holding his wife's hand over a skull. The wife leaned on an hourglass, with a daughter in black and white above, and below there were eleven children kneeling in rows, five of them plump figures in nightdress and six in ghostly drapes. "I find that most unsettling," she admitted, her finger pointed to the latter.

"Is there no legend hereabouts to explain it?"

"Dozens of them, and I find none of them acceptable." She gave a shudder. "Shall we start for home?" When they emerged from the church they were greeted by Allison and Walter Dodge, a brother and sister whom Diana had known since her childhood.

Alma watched the meeting curiously, for there was that in Walter Dodge's expression when he gazed on Diana which intrigued him. It was not difficult to see that Dodge was in love with Diana; and although Diana spoke warmly to him and teased the two with the ease of long affection, it was just as obvious that she did not return his regard. He heard Diana issue an invitation to her friends, "For we will need company, with George scurrying off for London the day after he arrives, and Lord Alma unable to ride due to an accident. Will you come tomorrow? Mrs. Lewis is arriving this asfternoon to stay with me and I should not like to throw her into a fret her first afternoon."

After the Dodges agreed to present themselves the following morning, the two groups diverged. Diana set an easy pace, but Alma's limp became more pronounced when they had still a half-mile to walk. "I am sorry you're in pain, Lord Alma," she said suddenly. "I have underestimated how fatiguing the walk to the village is."

She did not like the drawn look about his face, but she knew that he was determined to continue until he dropped. Abruptly she drew the shawl from about her shoulders and laid it on the path. They could not be seen because of the dense growth of the trees, newly coming into leaf, and she seated herself on an edge of the shawl.

Alma gazed at her in astonishment and his mouth tightened. "I am perfectly capable of continuing our walk, Miss Savile."

"Oh, don't be a gudgeon! What do you think it will prove to me or you if you continue to walk until you fall on your face? Do you want me to see that happen?"

"It will not happen."

"Certainly not, because you are going to lie down right now." When he continued to regard her obstinately she continued, "I have no intention of leaving this spot until you have rested. Please?"

Exasperated, he gazed at her for a moment and then abruptly stretched himself full-length on his stomach on the shawl. He refused to look at her, and she began to hum a song softly, accompanied by the bird calls about them. His exhaustion overcame him and it was an hour before he awoke, refreshing and angry.

"Why did you let me sleep?" he protested.

"Why not? Are we in a hurry to be back?" She folded the damp shawl and tucked it under her arm as they continued their walk. "Shall I tell you what I think about when I sit quietly for a while?" he grumbled, caught between curiosity and annoyance.

"I think about all the things I *don't* know, and the things that I don't even know I don't know," she laughed. "And then I decide what I shall concentrate on learning next, and I wonder whether there will be anything about it in our library. George has a marvellous library, of course, but it cannot begin to satisfy my curiosity on certain subjects. Then I have to go to Cambridge to see what I can find. Do you like to wander through stores where they have old books? It is quite a hobby of mine."

Alma looked rather startled. "What sorts of things are you curious about, Miss Savile?"

"Different things at different times. When I was younger I wanted to know the names of all the trees and plants that grew in the Park. Then I started to help Mr. Thatcher and I became very interested in medicine. Once, when we had an accident on the road, I wished to learn about road repair. There is a blind gentleman in Yorkshire, a Mr. John Metcalf, who is especially noted for his construction of roads and bridges. Imagine being sightless and knowing how to build roads over marshes!"

"How thoroughly do you study each of the subjects you choose, Miss Savile?"

"Oh, not so much as you probably suppose. I know a tiny bit about many things, but I never seem to finish studying something before a new interest crops up and I have abandoned my previous one. I am rather shatter-brained about it, I fear, but I enjoy it all the same."

"Did you decide on something new to study while you waited for me to wake up?" he asked, a note of bitterness creeping into his voice.

"I did not wait for you, Lord Alma. I could have gone on to the Park had I wished. Actually, when I am thinking about all those possibilities for learning something new, I quite forget where I am. Did you picture me sitting there impatient to be on my way and annoyed with you for holding me back?" When he did not answer her, she smiled shyly at him and said, "I hope you will forgive me, but I forgot all about you until you spoke to me."

Alma laughed then said, "Oh, I believe you, Miss Savile, and you are forgiven, but you did not answer my question. Have you decided on something new to study?"

"Well, I cannot decide between the birds or the times when Nicholas Paris lived," she said thoughtfully. "I've never finished my study of birds, but I am intrigued by what life was like in 1427. Do you know anything about that period?"

"Yes, more than I wish to," he confessed. "Shall I

29

send to Stillings for some books for you? I studied the period when I was up at Oxford."

"Did you? And you would send for some of your books?"

"Certainly. You could study birds until they arrive," he said, laughter dancing in his eyes.

"You are as bad as George, Lord Alma," she sighed. "Are you not curious about things? George translates Greek and Latin sometimes, but I must confess that I would rather simply read the same works in my own language for I have never mastered another."

"Not even French?" he asked, surprised.

"I can speak a few phrases, but my governess despaired of me and settled for globes instead. I have a solid knowledge of geography."

"Thank heaven. How would one survive without a knowledge of geography?" he teased. "What a strange combination you are—an archer, a student of geography, a fencer, an assistant apothecary . . ."

"I am ashamed of myself," she admitted seriously." "I do not seem to be able to study anything long enough to understand it really thoroughly. I once asked Cook to teach me about preparing foods and I worked at it for some time, but I became distracted by an interest in archeology. Cook did not speak to me for several weeks except when necessary. But I can plan a menu better now, and I should not starve if I had to provide for myself, so I suppose it was worth the time and trouble with Cook. George told you I fence with him sometimes?"

Alma, bewildered by the rapid change of subject, nodded his head.

"And you will fence with me? I could teach you archery in exchange . . . if you were interested," she said, the latter part of the sentence becoming more hesitant as she eyed him dubiously.

"It would be my pleasure," he found himself replying, much to his own surprise. Well, he had conceived an interest in seeing her fencing outfit, if George was so impressed with it.

She smiled warmly at him. "Thank you, Lord Alma, you are generous." As they approached the Park, Diana pointed out to him the features of the estate which had been her domain for so many years. The Park was set on a small green incline surrounded by lush lawns and vigorous forest growth of pines and oak. The house itself was of warm tan stone mellowed over two centuries to a richness in keeping with its setting. Deer grazed near the Home Wood and the hedges were filled with game. The kitchen gardens behind the house were extensive and well cared for, the balustraded terraces and flower gardens no less so. Parts of the stables were as ancient as the house, the rest more modern but architecturally in keeping with their predecessors. Diana could see beyond to the meadows and pastures, to her archery range and the orchards. Although it could not be seen because of the trees which flourished on its banks, the river ran through the Park, and opposite the river, also out of sight, was the stud farm.

Diana turned to Alma uncertainly. "Luncheon is at one. Shall you join me?"

"I cannot sit . . ."

"Never mind. We shall stand at the sideboard and eat with our fingers," she suggested gaily.

"Then I shall join you, Miss Savile." As Alma turned away in the hall, he thought about what George had said the previous evening. If one considered the strange Miss Savile as a younger brother, one was indeed no longer blue-devilled. He could not imagine why the Dodge fellow was in love with her; he felt sure there was not an ounce of the coquette in her diminutive figure. In fact, there was no resemblance to any woman he had ever known, and he had known a goodly number of them, he thought complacently. Still, as a younger brother she would do very well, as she was obviously intent on entertaining him. He had not fenced for months.

chapter four

Mrs. Lewis arrived at the Park midway through the afternoon, having had to return to her cottage once to check that the fire was out. Diana welcomed her and saw that she was settled in her room, done in shades of blue which delighted the old woman. When Mrs. Lewis was introduced to Lord Alma, she was puzzled that he continued to stand, and although he urged her to seat herself she was too much in awe of his title to do so. Therefore she continued to stand, even though she became weary and disgruntled. Diana had disappeared on a domestic errand and returned to find the two of them eyeing each other skeptically. Her lips quivered as she said, "You must be seated, Mrs. Lewis. Lord Alma is unable to do so, owing to his accident."

Neither of the two seemed satisfied with this explanation, but Mrs. Lewis eventually seated herself when Diana did, and Lord Alma left for his room. Because the day had chilled somewhat, Diana asked that a fire be laid on the hearth, and she adjusted the horse screen to Mrs. Lewis' pleasure before drawing up to her an elaborate worktable with a fabric-hung workbox drawer. Aware of the old lady's passion for embroidery, Diana assisted her to unpack the materials which went with her everywhere in an effort to keep her restless fingers busy.

"I hope you will excuse me, Mrs. Lewis. Lord Alma, being unable to ride, takes a bit of amusing." She grinned mischievously. "I intend to teach him some archery while he is here."

"Do you, my dear? How kind of you. Don't let me hold you back for I have plenty here to keep me occupied until dinner," Mrs. Lewis replied cheerily as she set to work, immediately forgetting Diana's presence altogether.

When Diana had sent a footman to enquire whether Lord Alma would join her on the archery range, she locked the dog Rogue in the stables, where she stressed the necessity of keeping him until she returned. The stable boy who had released him the previous day flushed and promised to make sure no future escape would take place.

Diana surveyed the contents of her archery shed— the bows and arrows, the pieces of leather for finger and arm guards. After setting aside her own equipment, she chose a larger bow and longer arrows for Alma. When he arrived she asked him to test the draw, a matter which he did awkwardly, never having handled a bow before. She demonstrated for him and taught him to brace the bow for herself. While demonstrating the proper stance and nocking procedure, she swept her long skirts behind her with a deft movement which amused her companion. Indeed, as he had decided, there was not the least bit of coquetry in her action. Diana, unaware of his thoughts, taught him to hold and draw properly, to use an anchor point and the relaxed attitude with which one must release the arrow once it was properly aimed.

Accustomed to excelling at all forms of sport in which he participated, Alma expected archery to prove no exception. Ignoring Diana's warning to use guards for his fingers and arm, he was vastly irritated with himself and her, when he was stung by the bowstring after he had released his first arrow, which came nowhere near the target.

"Confound it, Miss Savile, you are determined to kill me," he barked.

"You moved your elbow, Lord Alma."

"Well, you didn't tell me not to."

Diana handed him the guards he had refused previously and he accepted them, though he glowered at her menacingly. While he was attaching them, she called his attention to her own method of handling the bow; her arrow landed precisely in the center of the target.

"Remarkable!" he exclaimed admiringly, forgetting his grievance. After several attempts he began to hit the target with a fair degree of accuracy.

"Well done, Lord Alma. You will make an excellent archer in no time."

"Miss Savile," he said ominously, "These arrows we're using, they are not like the one you took from me."

Diana flushed guiltily. "No, these are target arrows. I . . . was using hunting arrows yesterday. I . . . wanted to see whether I would be as accurate with them."

Surprisingly, Alma's frown became an amused grin, and he shook his head wonderingly. "Just my luck to arrive when you were curious."

"Yes, it was very unfortunate," she sighed, her eyes laughing. "You're a good sport, Lord Alma. Would you like to see Crusader now?"

Alma was becoming familiar with her rapid changes of subject. "Yes, he should be exercised. I have scheduled a match between him and Barrymore's Chanticleer at the Spring Meetings, and I sent my groom ahead to London. Have you anyone who can handle him?"

"I can manage him if he's well-mannered," she suggested hesitantly.

He eyed her skeptically. "You are very small for so large an animal, if you will excuse my saying so."

"You know that doesn't signify if he's well-trained," she protested.

"And if I say he's not well-trained you will wonder why I own him," he grumbled, uneasily running a hand through his black hair.

"If you do not wish me to ride him, I shall not. Why not come to the stables and you can watch me," Although her eyes beseeched him, she spoke diffidently.

"Very well."

They returned the archery equipment to the shed and proceeded to the stables, where Diana released Rogue. In an ecstacy of delight the dog nearly knocked her over, and Alma again expressed his doubts of her ability to control Crusader.

Regardless, Diana ordered the horse saddled and wandered around the stables with Alma during the wait pointing out the horses bred at the Park. When Crusader was ready, Jenkins spoke confidently to his mistress. "He's pretty-behaved, Miss Diana. I misdoubt me you will have any trouble with him."

She nodded and allowed him to hand her into the saddle, all the while a whisper of encouragement to the horse on her lips. The dappled stallion fidgetted momentarily but obeyed the firm hand on his reins. After she had ridden him about in the immediate vicinity of the stables for a few minutes, she turned questioning eyes to Alma. He nodded brusquely.

It was unnecessary to urge the stallion to the gallop. Her first indication that she would hold him in no longer was responded to by a rapid lengthening of his stride. Although Diana had ridden horses all her life, magnificent beasts as were always housed at the Park, she had never been on so powerful an animal. The speed he gained caused the wind to knock her bonnet back onto her shoulders; her hair whipped against her face almost blinding her for a moment. She was afraid to raise a hand to brush it back lest she lose control of him. They were rapidly approaching a fence, and, for a moment, her heart failed her; but the very enthusiasm with which Crusader approached it gave her courage, and they sailed over it like drifting birds.

Diana gently reined in the horse and he responded immediately. When she had him at a walk, she secured the bonnet on her head once more, the recalcitrant lock of hair firmly imprisoned beneath. They retraced their paths to the stables at a more leisurely gait and she allowed Alma to lift her down, his eyebrows raised in query.

"I have never ridden such a horse, and it was very exciting, but I shall not do so again. He is too much for me, as you said." She bit her lip unhappily as she handed the reins to Jenkins.

"You were frightened." Alma asked gently.

Her lips quivered slightly and she nodded. "My bonnet came off and with my hair in my eyes I couldn't see well. I cannot remember when I have ever been afraid on a horse before, and George had me riding almost before I could walk." There was a suspicion of moisture in her eyes.

"It is nothing to be ashamed of, Miss Savile," he said hearteningly. "I should not have allowed you to ride him. I had forgotten the first time I rode him . . ."

"What happened?"

He gave an embarrassed laugh. "I was very sure of myself, you know. He was bred for racing but I was determined to buy him. I was very nearly knocked off when I jumped him over a style too near a tree and a branch lashed me so hard I almost lost my seat. I am accustomed to him now, of course, and had forgotten how unsettling his power can be." He smiled down at her, pleased to see that the moisture in her eyes had disappeared.

"Perhaps Jenkins can exercise him, or Walter, when he comes to visit."

"Walter?"

"Walter Dodge. You met him this morning in the village. He and his sister are to come tomorrow."

Alma indeed remembered the love-sick Walter. "You think he will be able to handle Crusader?"

"Certainly, but I will caution him. He is very seldom so cocksure as to make a mistake."

Although Diana said this with no intention of deprecation, Alma eyed her sharply. No, he did not believe she was mocking him, or even herself, but merely making a statement of fact. "I take it the Dodges live nearby?"

"Yes, their land marches with George's to the east. They are quite a large family. Walter is the eldest, and then two brothers who are at Cambridge, then Allison with another two sisters following. Mr. and Mrs. Dodge are the best of neighbors, forever enlisting the large landholders in efforts to reduce the suffering in the neighborhood. George is mostly from home, but he trusts me to use my discretion in assisting in their projects."

She fell silent as she remembered the last such endeavor and its outcome of an offer from Walter. It had disturbed her to disappoint the young man, but she really could see no purpose in marrying him. She was entirely satisfied with her life, and she had yet to meet someone who would accept her as she was. Even Walter, for all his devotion, frowned on her diverse interests, which she could not see harmed anyone. Only her brother George understood and accepted her, she thought with a sigh, and that was probably because nothing and no one seemed to upset his equable nature.

Alma had attempted to question Diana further on the Dodges but, finding her so engrossed in her thoughts that she did not hear him, he gazed down at her (she only came up to his chest), and shrugged. She looked the image of a village schoolmistress in her loose gray riding dress, her hair pulled severely back to the nape of her neck. Strange that she dressed so unfashionably when her brother was the picture of elegance. Rigged out properly, she would probably be presentable, he mused. Ah well, it was no doubt the exile in the country which left her so lamentably ignorant of London modality. George really should see that she had some decent clothes though, Alma thought. It would not do to have one's sister taken for a governess!

Alonna Sanfield left London on the day her engagement was announced, and she did not intend to return until her father had the announcement retracted. In fact, she was not sure that she would be able to return at all. It had not been so very difficult to come into London society in the fall when she had her sister to guide her and when everything was unique and interesting to her. The little season, too, had made the demands on her less than they would have been in the spring, but her sister was in the country now, near Colchester, expecting the arrival of her second child momentarily. There was only an aging, imperious aunt in London to chaperone her, a woman who would not be the least sympathetic to her plight.

Although she sought her father to discuss with him her decision to leave town, he was not in the house and had not indicated where he was headed. Callers arrived regularly and were turned away, but the insistent thump of the knocker began to wear Alonna down. She repaired to the library, where she wrote her father a note explaining that she was going to her sister Margaret until the announcement was withdrawn and there had been time for the gossip to die down. A nine days' wonder, she hoped, and she begged her father to understand and to send her a copy of the retraction as soon as it appeared.

A footman was instructed to purchase her ticket on the Norwich Mail as far as Colchester. When he had left she advised her maid that she wished the girl to accompany her to her sister's for a while, and to be ready to depart early that evening. Lord Franston did not return before it was time for Alonna to depart; unsure whether this pleased or depressed her, she arrived at the General Post Office in Lombard Street well before the eight o'clock departure. She had never seen so many of the maroon and black coaches with their scarlet wheels all in one place. The Royal coat of arms on the doors made them very impressive, as did the guard in his Royal scarlet livery, ready to mount to the boot to protect the locked mail box.

There were only two other inside passengers, a young man who was dressed neatly but not fashionably, and an old woman who grumbled continually, not one word of which discourse could be understood by the young women. Immediately the guard's horn was heard, the coach started with a lurch and Alonna gazed forlornly out the window. Her maid, Drucy, was evidently thrilled by the whole scene in the yard and kept up a constant stream of chatter as they clattered through London and out into the countryside. It was dark already and the night outside London seemed overwhelmingly black after the lights of the city. Alonna silently watched the ghostly shapes of trees move past the window and allowed the swaying of the coach to lull her to sleep.

It was close to midnight when the mail reached Colchester. The landlord at the Three Horseshoes was willing enough for Alonna to hire a post chaise to take her to Trafford Hall, but not until morning, and she was not eager to spend another two hours on the road at that time of night in any case, so she took rooms for her maid and herself and asked to be called early. The emotional and physical exhaustion of the day thrust sleep upon her the minute her head touched the pillow.

Diana was not able to convince Alma to take dinner with her and Mrs. Lewis, but he joined them for a while in the music room in the evening. Mrs. Lewis, unable to comprehend the full extent of his injury, felt uncomfortable having him stand. This caused Diana some amusement, but she could see that he was disgruntled and she bid him turn her music for her while she played. This gave him an excuse to stand by the harpsichord, but it was not easy to cajole him into a better frame of mind; the longer he lived with his injury, the more it was borne in on him how much it inconvenienced him. He had spent his adult years going where he wished to go and doing what he wished to do. He was attractive, possessed of a handsome fortune and flourishing estates, and was much in demand in society. The fact that one action of a minute chit could debilitate him so enormously made his spleen rise. He glowered down at Diana as she concentrated on the keyboard, her voice sweetly singing of the month of May.

Raising her eyes to his, she smiled apologetically. It was not difficult for her to understand how he felt, but there was little she could do about it. Only time would heal his wound, and then he would perhaps forget the inconvenience as he picked up the threads of his normal life again. "Tell me what is your favorite, Lord Alma, and we shall sing a duet for Mrs. Lewis."

The old woman beamed on them and, in spite of his reluctance, Alma refused to be so rude as to ignore his hostess's suggestion. His rich baritone was uncertain at first, gradually becoming stronger as he shrugged off his annoyance and entered into the spirit of the madrigal they sang. Without prompting he proposed the next song, and a pleasant half hour was spent by the three of them until he began to feel the strain of standing. Too proud to admit his weakness, he irritably shifted from foot to foot. Not now or at any time would he speak of his fatigue; he was, after all, a sportsman

Diana closed her music and turned to Mrs. Lewis. "I am ready for my bed."

Mrs. Lewis, who was nothing if not biddable, rose quickly and stuffed away the embroidery she had been working on. "Yes, it has been a busy day," she murmured, "and very productive."

Intent on proving there was no hurry about his departure, Alma bowed them out of the room with lightly veiled sarcasm in his wishes that Diana spend a good night. He heard her muffled laughter as the door closed behind her. When their footsteps had died away, he took himself rapidly to his room where his valet had a great deal of trouble undressing him, as he refused to rise from the bed for this service.

Although the thought of a boiled fowl was not entirely appealing, George Savile headed for White's in St. James's Street when he arrived in London. Few of the clubs, for all their claim to companionship, could offer a decent meal. While he waited for his food he absently picked up the current issue of the *Herald* to thumb through it with little interest. When he had read the announcement with a mixture of incredulity and distress, he felt little inclined for the meal which was served him, but proceeded to devour it, since his body had been denied sufficient sustenance at midday.

George was hailed by friends and reluctantly agreed to join them at the newest gambling hall. His mind, however, was concentrated on the problem of whether he should seek an interview with Alonna in light of the announcement. Every rule of society and common sense told him that he should not, but he could not bear the thought of leaving matters as they stood. There was something in their relationship, he was sure of it. Ordinarily rather quiet, Alonna had seemed to blossom when he spoke with her; the attractive face would become animated and the blue eyes sparkle. George did not have a particularly high opinion of Lord Vallert, though he did not know him well. Still, he himself had never indicated his intentions to Alonna, and she might have thought it necessary to accept this offer of marriage.

When he had broken even at faro, he quitted his companions in spite of their protests. The servants at his town house had been alerted by his valet to expect him, so he quietly greeted the butler and went straight to his bedchamber. During his restless night he finally convinced himself that he would call on Miss Sanfield the next morning to offer his felicitations, and to assess her feelings if he were able.

chapter five

Assuming that Lord Alma would sleep late the next morning, Diana took her favorite mare out for an early gallop. On her return she found Alma in the stables talking with Jenkins about Crusader, and though he eyed her somewhat resentfully, he assisted her from her mount with great courtesy.

"Have you broken your fast, Lord Alma?" she asked.

"No. I thought to have a r—walk first."

"Would you like to walk over to the stud farm with me? I cannot think George had time to visit it, and, if there are questions, you would know better than I how to answer them."

Alma was annoyed that she always suggested a project which would interest him. If she had proposed a round of archery at this hour he would have been able to reject the idea with haughty disdain. He felt like a sulky child; his only desire at times was to snub her and make her pay for his discomfort. However, he *did* want to see George's stud farm, so he nodded curtly and assumed a distracted air so that she would not expect him to speak with her.

In high spirits after her ride, with the smell of spring in the air, buds bursting out on the trees and the birds singing cheerfully, Diana's gaze took in the well-manicured fields, the dense Home Wood and the lanes curving through the countryside further away. She began to hum a tune.

Desperately as Alma wished to ignore her, he was enchanted by the melody and found himself asking her what it was.

"Well, I have never precisely named it, but it is about spring."

"You wrote it?"

"Yes, I do that sometimes when I am particularly happy."

"But not when you are sad?" he asked mockingly, his black eyebrows lifted.

"I am rarely sad," she admitted frankly. "I imagine if I were I would compose a song to fit my mood."

"I see," he replied, though he was not at all sure he did. "Does your song have words?"

"Yes, shall I teach them to you?"

To his own astonishment Alma soon found himself singing a duet with his companion as they wandered across the fields toward the stud farm. When they arrived at the stable, lads greeted Diana and she introduced Alma as a friend of her brother's. She had not seen the most recent acquisition to the stud and was curious as to why they were handling him so cautiously.

"He's very nearly wild, ma'am," one of the men explained as the magnificent black struck out with a foreleg at his assistant, who neatly dodged it.

Alma approached the black at a discreet distance, his voice softened to murmur soothing words. The black pricked his ears forward and seemed to grow more quiet. Fascinated by this show of affinity, Diana stepped forward to join Alma by the horse; his voice was soft but authoritative when he ordered, "Stay back, Miss Savile."

Immediately obeying him, she retreated to her former position. The black had grown restless again and the groom holding his bridle had all he could do to hang on. Alma stretched out an imperative hand to the groom, who reluctantly released the bridle for him to grasp. The viscount started his low-voiced commentary to the horse again and began to lead him about the stable yard with frequent stops and starts and turns which the horse nervously followed. Horrified, Diana watched as he swung himself up onto the unsaddled beast. She saw his face pale as his bottom met the horse's flanks, but the determination in his eyes froze on her lips the protest she had meant to offer. The black pranced and bucked for a moment until the stream of words from his rider soothed him again. Alma dug his booted heels into the horse's sides and allowed him a short, restrained gallop before returning to the stable yard and swinging himself to the ground. He then handed the horse to the groom (who had watched this performance in amazement) and turned to Diana. "I am ready for breakfast," he said blandly.

Diana bit her lip and nodded. They walked back to the Park without a word, and Alma took his meal in his room; Diana in the dining parlor with Mrs. Lewis.

George Savile found that his decision to seek an interview with Alonna Sanfield was not to prove easy. He could not call until a decent hour and when he did so he was informed that Miss Sanfield was not at home. George then instructed the butler to advise Miss Sanfield that he would return during the afternoon, but the impassive-faced butler assured him that Miss Sanfield would not be home during the afternoon, so George exasperatedly said that he would call the next day, in that case. The butler informed him that Miss Sanfield would not be home then, either.

"Is Miss Sanfield out of town?" George finally asked.

"Yes, sir."

"And when do you expect her return?"

"I have no idea, sir."

"Is Lord Franston available?"

"No, sir, his lordship is out."

"Is he also out of town?"

"No, sir."

"Then do you know when I may call to find him available?"

"No, sir. He has not been receiving callers since yesterday." The butler kept his eyes locked on a point somewhere above George's head.

"Might I enquire if Miss Sanfield has returned to Hampshire?"

"I would not be at liberty to say, sir."

George seldom felt ruffled by anyone or anything, but he would have liked to shake the smooth-voiced butler until he obtained the information he desired. Instead he turned on his heels and left, all the while trying to decide how he could get in touch with Alonna and whether it would do him any good to do so.

He repaired to White's and kept an ear open for the current *on dit* in the hopes that he would learn something of value. After spending several hours nursing two glasses of brandy and being bored by the usual run of gossip imparted by the various members drifting in and out, he finally overheard something of interest.

Carlton Boothe, slightly drunk from the three glasses of wine he had downed in rapid succession, leaned confidentially toward his companion, Geoffrey Walthers, and slurred, "Heard Vallert's 'tended's given him the slip. Left town soon's the 'nouncem'nt came out. Vallert's sister went to call yest'day aft'noon and learned the little lady's not in town. But she was there the day b'fore," he said knowingly, " 'cause I saw her m'self."

When the two men progressed to new fields of defamation, George paid his reckoning and departed. He could waste more time trying to track down Lord Franston, or he could go in search of Alonna, which could easily also be a waste of time. George was aware of the location of Lord Franston's estate in Hampshire but he had no way of knowing if Alonna had headed there or not. It seemed the likeliest of possibilities, however, and he determined to pursue it.

It was late afternoon before he was ready to depart and his valet, astonished to see such activity from his ordinarily languid employer, decried the necessity of setting off at such an hour.

"I'm not taking you, Stephen. I have a lot of ground to cover and perhaps more than I bargain for. It will be most uncomfortable and you will enjoy the leisure of London, I feel sure."

"Not coming with you? But, sir, you always take me with you!" the valet wailed.

"Not this time. I may be gone for several days, but I shall send word if it becomes longer than that."

When Stephen had seen the portmanteau stashed in the back of the phaeton and George jumped up and grasped the reins from the groom, the valet was even more astonished. "You surely will be taking the groom at least!"

"No, I go alone this time." George gave the horses their heads in so far as it was possible in the London traffic and breathed a sigh of relief to be at last making some move. With changes at Brentford and Hounslow he made The Bush in Staines within a few hours, but the sky was overcast and foretold of rain, so he settled there for the night. In the morning he awoke to a pouring rain which made it impossible for him to set out in his open carriage. He debated the efficacy of hiring a closed carriage, but decided against it. The rain did not let up all day, and there was word of flooding on the Exeter Road to cheer him.

Lord Franston had been more than a little annoyed when he read his daughter's note. In spite of her plea he had no intention of approaching Vallert to have him withdraw the announcement, nor of doing so himself. He had seen four of her older brothers and sisters safely married off; Alonna was the last of them and he was intent on seeing the business settled once and for all. If Vallert wanted to marry her, he could have her. Not such a bad fellow, either. There was no reason why Alonna should refuse him, and she would thank her father in the future for his patience with her.

Ever since the announcement had appeared, Vallert himself had been a prey to misgivings. When his friends began to congratulate him and mere acquaintances stopped him in the street to express their knowledge of his impending marriage, he suddenly realized what he had done. If Miss Sanfield refused to marry him now he would be a laughingstock. With some trepidation he took himself to the Franston town house the day after the announcement appeared, only to be informed, as George Savile had been an hour previously, that Miss Sanfield was not at home.

Vallert, however, knew precisely where to find Lord Franston at this hour of the day, and he repaired to Batson's Coffee House in Cornhill where he knew the old boy would be smoking his pipe and reading the papers.

Batson's was a favorite meeting place for such as Lord Franston, and Vallert had been obliged to meet him there, rather than at his home, several days previously when he had sought to pay his addresses to Franston's daughter. The old man was happily blowing his cloud in exactly the same chair Vallert had found him in on that other occasion.

"Lord Franston, I would have a word with you if I may," he said crisply in an attempt to gain the upper hand from the start.

"Ah, Vallert. Have a seat, young man," Lord Franston offered with a negligent wave of his hand toward a chair covered with newspapers.

The younger man removed these and seated himself as carelessly as was possible without indicating disrespect for his prospective father-in-law. "I attempted to call on Miss Alonna this morning and was told that she was not at home," he said accusingly.

"Very true, dear boy. She has gone to her sister. About to have a child, you know."

"*Who* is about to have a child?" Vallert asked, astonished.

"M'daughter Margaret, of course. Alonna says she will not have you. Very upset about the announcement you put in the papers. Must have made a mull of asking her, young man," he grunted, with a piercing look at his companion.

Vallert waved the objection aside. "It is merely a maiden's shyness. I feel sure that now the engagement is announced she will see the reasonableness of going through with it."

"Much as I feel myself," Franston agreed.

"She should not have left town just now when we should be seen together," Vallert pointed out aggrievedly.

"Well, go and bring her back," her father suggested as he calmly drew on his pipe.

"So I shall," Vallert pronounced, bristling. "Where is she?"

"I told you, with her sister."

"And where does her sister *reside?*" Vallert asked with exaggerated patience.

"Near Colchester. Trafford Hall they call it. Fancy place but not at all to my liking."

"I shall tell her you sent me to fetch her," Vallert suggested slyly.

"Good idea. Not one to disobey her own father, that girl. When will you leave?"

"Tomorrow. I have an engagement this evening with some friends, but you can look for us the day after, I have no doubt."

"Indeed." Franston smiled earnestly at the younger man. "Make sure you don't muff it this time, my boy."

Vallert did not consider this remark worth responding to. He bowed to the old man and took himself off feeling much better than he had since the announcement had appeared. Miss Alonna was mistaken when she said that her father's permission was no more than that; the old man obviously intended that Vallert should have her whether she desired it or not.

chapter six

Alonna's first thought on awakening at the inn was that perhaps today the retraction had appeared, if her father had gone to the Catherine Street office of the *Herald* the previous afternoon. No, probably it would be another day before it appeared, and even longer before she held it in her own hands. She sighed as Drucy assisted her into her long-sleeved, full-skirted blue muslin. Drucy left her in the dining parlor; the maid took her own meal in the noisy, bustling kitchen. Alonna shyly surveyed the room with its blazing fire and cheerful red curtains. She had never stayed at an inn with only a maid before but she did not wish to behave as though it were a new experience, so she seated herself and ordered a cup of chocolate and toast from the rosy-cheeked serving girl who approached her. There were a number of other occupants in the room, each intent on his meal, and not a glance was directed at her.

When the landlord came to inform her that the post chaise would be ready in half an hour, she thanked him and dawdled over her meager meal, stretching it over the necessary period of time. She paid the reckoning and sent for her maid as though it were a matter of course. Nothing raised her courage so well as imagining that George Savile was watching her as she climbed into the carriage. Soon the landscape began to look vaguely familiar, for she had visited her sister several years previously for a summer.

Once through the gates Alonna could see the ridiculous but loveable mushroom-shaped shrubs which dotted the space before Trafford Hall. The Hall itself was a courtyard house with its entrance in the side of one of the two projections on the main front. There were five-sided, square and plump semicircular bays parading across the front, and steep, finialed gables which vied with battlements and tall, slender chimney stacks. The house was close to two hundred years old and its façade had not been altered in any way. Even the stone-mullioned windows remained. Alonna had never been so pleased to arrive at any place in her life.

The postillions were paid and the post chaise dismissed before the butler arrived at the front door to ascertain who had arrived. He recognized Alonna immediately from her earlier stay in the house, and his astonishment was quickly masked. While she and Drucy were shown into the hall, a maid was sent to prepare rooms for them.

"Lady Trafford is at home, is she not, Lake?" Alonna asked anxiously.

"She has just been brought to bed, Miss Sanfield. We were not expecting you, were we?"

"No," she laughed. "I will go to her at once if the doctor permits. Perhaps I can be of use to her."

Though he did not say so, the butler doubted the possibility, but led her to her sister's bedchamber where she found her brother-in-law and the doctor in the dressing room. Lord Trafford started when he saw her and the doctor looked aggrieved at her sudden advent.

"Phillip, I hope all is well with Margaret," she burst out anxiously.

"Alonna! Where have you sprung from? Yes, Margaret is coming along fine, but Dr. Newton has just advised me that we are about to have twins."

"How splendid! And Mark—is he well?"

"Lord Trafford smiled. "Yes, but he is very anxious to hear news of his new brother or sister."

Alonna turned her gaze to Dr. Newton as her brother-in-law introduced her. "I do not wish to be in the way, Doctor, but if there is anything I can do to help I hope you will allow me."

The doctor regarded her with more tolerance than when she had entered the room. "I feel sure your sister would welcome your presence for a few minutes. You may go in to her if you wish."

The bedchamber was darkened and her sister Margaret lay on the enormous fourposter with a maid sponging her brow. As blond as her sister, and usually as well-groomed, Margaret's hair was now in disarray and the blue eyes were not so alert and sparkling as usual.

"Margaret, it is Alonna."

Margaret turned her head toward the door and her face broke into a smile which delighted her sister. "Oh, Alonna, how good it is to see you! Tilda was to have come but she has been indisposed these last two weeks, and Phillip's mother is not due until tomorrow." She gasped as a wave of pain engulfed her.

In a moment Alonna was taking her sister's hand in a gentle clasp. When Margaret's face cleared again, she said encouragingly, "I hear you are about to produce two children, you clever girl."

Margaret giggled. "Is Phillip stunned? Dr. Newton will not allow him in here."

"He seemed a trifle overcome, but I could not tell if it was because of the twins or my arrival."

"Why are you come, love? Is Papa with you?"

"No, he is in town. I wanted to get away from London for a space," Alonna said carefully, "and there was nowhere I would rather come than to you. The babies are a little early, are they not?"

Stoically enduring another wave of discomfort, Margaret was unable to answer for a moment. "Dr. Newton says it is often the case with twins. Tell me what you've been doing."

Alonna drew a chair up to the bed and regaled her sister with stories of her activities in town, with never a mention of Vallert's proposal. She paused each time her sister cried out or clenched her hand, only to continue again when the pain had passed. Eventually Dr. Newton came into the room to examine his patient and indicated that Alonna should leave.

Margaret turned to her with wistful eyes and Alonna smiled. "I shall stay, Doctor, since Margaret wishes it."

A formidable frown creased his brow. "Lady Trafford, your sister is . . . young to witness such an event."

Guiltily, Margaret said with reluctance, "Perhaps he is right . . . I did not think." Another contraction seized her and her grip on Alonna's hand tightened.

Alonna sat calmly by her side, a hand soothing her sister's brow. "I shall not mind, my dear. Depend on me."

With an exasperated shrug, Dr. Newton desisted. Aristocratic ladies were not to be argued with. "It will not be long now, my lady." He turned to the maid and gave her some low-voiced instructions which sent her bustling from the room.

From the bedside table Alonna picked up a book and opened it to the leather marker. She read in an even voice, pausing when her hand was gripped painfully, and continuing when the hand relaxed. After a while there was a change in the movements of the woman beside her and Alonna looked questioningly at the doctor.

"She is about to push the babies out now. Put the book aside," he said gruffly.

For the next half hour Alonna encouraged her sister to do as the doctor instructed. Margaret seemed dazed with the effort and Alonna felt concerned for her, but Dr. Newton continued to guide her gently and imperturbably. Alonna gazed in wonder as he lifted a squalling infant, and a few minutes later another, and handed one to the maid and another to her, each child wrapped in a blanket.

"Oh, Margaret, they're beautiful," she gasped, the tears streaming down her cheeks. She handed the infant she held to her sister to see and Margaret smiled, weary but pleased. "This one is a girl."

"The other is a boy," Dr. Newton said, with an enormous grin. He proceeded to instruct the bathing of the babies and calmly explained what was happening when there was activity about Margaret once more.

When everything was quiet and a second cradle had been procured from the nursery, Phillip was allowed into the room to view his two new children. He went first to his wife, though, to sit by her and speak quietly, holding her hand. She had to urge him to leave her to see the babies, but her face was radiant when Alonna slipped from the room.

The housekeeper indicated the chamber which had

been prepared for her and promised to have a meal sent up directly. Alonna dropped into a chair in her room, exhausted by the strain of seeing her sister in pain and exhilarated by the miracle she had witnessed. A smile crept over her face and she laughed out loud at the pure joy of witnessing the arrival of a child, nay, two children, into the world. When there was a tap at the door, Drucy brought in a tray for her and proceeded to listen spellbound to her mistress's excited tale of the arrival of her newest nephew and niece.

Allison and Walter Dodge arrived at the Park at midmorning. Alma had put in no appearance since his return from the stud farm, so Diana sent a message to inform him that her guests had arrived if he would be interested in seeing them. Mrs. Lewis had wandered off to chat of their mutual acquaintances with the housekeeper, so Diana greeted the Dodges in the main parlor alone.

"Has Lord Alma left, Diana?" Allison asked, surprised.

"No, but he may be indisposed. He had an accident a few days ago and is unable to sit, which is very irksome," she said ruefully. "I had hoped that Walter might have a game of billiards with him. You cannot imagine how difficult it is to think up activities that do not involve seating oneself."

Allison giggled. "Does he come to meals?"

"Not usually, though we did eat at the sideboard at luncheon yesterday." She sighed. "I caused his accident, so he is none too happy with me."

For the first time Walter spoke, a martial light in his serious brown eyes. "That is not very polite of him. A gentleman should not hold a grudge against a lady."

"Well, Walter, if I were a total stranger to you and I shot you with an arrow, even you might be vexed with me."

Allison's eyes widened. "You shot him?"

"Yes, for he galloped behind my target just as Rogue jumped on me and made my arrow go astray. I do not blame Lord Alma for his irritation, nor for being sadly out of countenance, but there is so little I can do to keep him busy. George had invited him to stay for a few days but unexpectedly had to drive to London on urgent business." Diana gazed out the window thoughtfully and wondered if her brother was engaged by now.

There was a movement at the door and Diana glanced up to see Alma enter. He bowed formally to the Dodges and began a conversation with Allison, who was to leave for London with her brother and parents in a week's time to be introduced to London society; she was delighted to meet someone so well acquainted with the metropolis.

Walter welcomed the opportunity to speak with Diana. She had kindly but firmly refused his offer of marriage at Christmas, but he hoped that with time he would be able to overcome her reluctance. Diana trusted that he would meet someone to his liking while in London with his family and she had therefore determined on a ruthless course of assuring him that she would not change her mind. Only if he reached London with that understanding would he make some effort to enjoy the company of the young women he would meet there.

"I had hoped we might have a ride together today," he suggested as he awkwardly attempted to take snuff in an imitation of George's elegant manner.

"Perhaps later, Walter. I should prefer that you offer Lord Alma a game of billiards after a bit, and later you might like to ride his horse, Crusader. He allowed me to do so yesterday, but hesitantly, and he was quite right. I have never ridden a more powerful animal. I told him you would not be overconfident were you to try him."

"You intrigue me," Walter admitted as he sneezed. "I have never known you to have the least problem with a well-mannered horse."

"Oh, Crusader is perfectly trained, and his speed is exhilarating. I am sure you would enjoy your ride."

When Allison and Alma joined them, Walter obligingly suggested a game of billiards. Alma cast a questioning glance at Diana, who said, "Yes, you two go along. Allison and I have some things to discuss."

After they had left the room Allison chuckled. "I found it disconcerting to stand the whole time we were talking. It's a pity he cannot sit."

"Yes, Mrs. Lewis feels it, too, but it will not be for so very long."

"Do you think he will go to London when he is recovered?" Allison asked hopefully.

"Yes, he and George had been planning to go there after a short stay here and I have no doubt that he will leave the moment he can sit comfortably in a carriage for a few hours. You will probably see both him and George in London while you're there. Now tell me how your plans progress."

While the young women discussed the only topic which engrossed Allison's interest of late, the two men found their skills at billiards well-matched and enjoyed several games. They carried on a desultory conversation during which Walter decided that Lord Alma was not such a bad fellow after all, and Alma decided that Walter was better than the usual country gentleman. Alma could give Walter five years, and he was not intent on developing their acquaintance into a friendship, but the younger man proved a better companion than he had expected. It made Alma all the more puzzled that Walter was obviously in love with Miss Savile, but there was no accounting for taste.

When the men rejoined them Diana announced that she had ordered an alfresco luncheon in the gardens. Walter obligingly stood with Alma during this repast while Diana and Allison seated themselves on the old stone benches and continued their discussion. Alma was surprised to learn that Allison, too, tried her hand at archery.

"It is one of our country sports for women hereabouts," Diana explained as they headed toward the archery range. "Walter, will you see that Rogue is locked up?"

Her suitor willingly attended to the small commission before joining the others. He and Diana formed a team against Allison and Alma, and since neither of the latter could compare with the former, they won handily.

This did not seem to distress either of the losers; in fact Alma was encouraged by his progress.

Diana took Alma aside for a moment as the equipment was being returned to the shed and asked, "Will you mind if Walter rides Crusader? I have suggested it to him, and I am sure you need have no fear of the horse coming to any grief."

"I bow to your judgment of his abilities, Miss Savile," he replied politely. "Will you all be riding now?"

Her eyes laughed at the forlorn note in his voice but she assured him that she would stay with him if he so desired. "I had thought you might wish a break, though, for your face is beginning to look pinched again."

He stiffened at this mention of his weakness and his stormy eyes glared at her as he replied, "I have not the slightest need for a rest, Miss Savile."

"Then you will wish for me to stay with you while Allison and Walter ride," she replied with mock disappointment.

"No, I will not. I am perfectly capable of entertaining myself for an hour."

"Excellent," she said cheerfully. "We shall have tea when we return."

Alma watched irritably as the other three mounted and rode out of the stable yard. Walter proved to be as capable as Miss Savile had predicted; there was no overconfidence in his handling of the powerful Crusader, but a healthy respect for the strength of the mount. When the three were out of sight Alma returned to his room and flung himself on his bed, exhausted.

While riding, Diana had the beginnings of an idea for keeping Lord Alma occupied during his stay. It was evident that the enforced disassociation from horses while he recuperated was the largest of his burdens. She had been appalled to see him mount the wild black that morning and wished for no further recurrence of such folly. Obviously he had not wished to pass up the perfect moment to mount the horse, but he had not aided the progress of his recovery by doing so.

When the three returned from their ride Diana took some time to speak with Jenkins, who was astonished by her idea but grudgingly admitted that it could probably be carried out. She instructed him to do so and inform her when he was finished. Although Alma joined her and the Dodges and Mrs. Lewis for tea somewhat refreshed by the nap he had inadvertently succumbed to, he disappeared again after the Dodges left, not to be seen for the rest of the day.

chapter seven

Diana took the precaution the next day of sending a message to Frank Edwards, Sir Lowell's son, inviting him to spend the afternoon at the Park if he was free. Frank was the best fencer in the area. It did not particularly please her to have to invite him because he was another of her local suitors and he was aggressively persistent in his importunings. Walter considered him negligible as a rival for Diana's hand—a frippery fellow carousing about the countryside when he was not living high in London. There was none of the solid, hard-working virtue Walter himself had to bring to Miss Savile. Frank led a life of pleasure, always dressed to the nines and ready for a lark. It must be admitted, of course, that he was exceedingly handsome, perhaps even intriguing, with his brooding air which gave place to laughing animation at the drop of a hat. Walter thought him loose in the haft; Diana found him annoying.

Mrs. Lewis shared a companionable breakfast with Diana after which she adjourned to the small parlor to work on her embroidery. The old woman considered it strange that Diana's guest kept so much to his room and she took to forgetting his presence at the Park at all, except when she remembered that he was her reason for being there. Diana sat with her for a while before sending a message to Alma that she planned to walk to the deer park if he would like to accompany her.

Now this was an invitation Alma could easily refuse, but it arrived when he was intolerably bored. He had spent the previous evening playing piquet with his valet and then reading a book he had sought from the library. When he had been in the library he had heard the sound of the harpsichord and Miss Savile's voice in song in the next room. Although he was tempted to join Mrs. Lewis and her there, he was determined that he would not be cajoled out of his black humor. He could have been in London at that very moment enjoying himself! His hand crept to his right buttock, which he had caused to bleed again that morning by his foolish action of riding the black horse. It exacerbated his temper rather than soothed it that Miss Savile had made no comment on his rashness. He chose a book at random and returned to his room to find that if he wished to read he might learn of the native plants of Cambridgeshire.

So Alma joined Diana for her walk to the deer park. He was resolved to appear pleasant this morning, ashamed of his churlishness. When the opportunity presented itself, he pointed out the plants he had read of the night before, being possessed of a wonderful memory for drawings. After he had identified several obscure plants correctly Diana turned to him in amazement.

"I had no idea you were so well-informed on our native oddities, Lord Alma."

Alma cursed himself for being a blatherskite. With a slight flush he remarked, "I happened to pick up a book in the library by mistake."

"Heavy going, I should imagine," she retorted with a grin. "I wonder that you bothered."

"I was bored," he said without thinking.

"I have invited Frank Edwards to visit this afternoon. He is the finest fencer in the area, besides George, and I had hoped you might enjoy having a bit of sport."

He turned to her guiltily. "I have not been a pleasant guest, Miss Savile, and I hope you will forgive me. I cannot understand why such a little inconvenience should so discompose me. I am used to being very active, you know, but I would not have you rack your brains for ways to amuse me."

"It is a challenge," she laughed, as she gathered some brilliantly yellow daffodils into the basket she carried. Her eyes were impish as she told him mysteriously, "I think I shall have a surprise ready for you tomorrow."

He regarded her dubiously. "What is it?"

"You shall have to wait and see. I am not altogether sure it will work out," she mused. In an effort to turn the conversation she treated him to some escapades of George's youth which soon had him laughing. They returned to the Park in charity with one another, but he did not join her for luncheon.

When Frank Edwards arrived Mrs. Lewis and Diana had settled in the small parlor. He bore with him the equipment he needed for fencing, since Diana had requested him to do so, but he was more intent on flattering her than on participating in the sport with Alma, who joined them shortly.

Mrs. Lewis regarded Edwards benignly, as did all of the old women of the neighborhood, since he adopted an exaggerated gallantry which was pleasing to them. Alma took an immediate dislike to him.

"I have had George's equipment set out for you, Lord Alma. I thought you might use the Long Gallery." Diana made no move to accompany them when they turned to depart.

"You don't come with us, Diana?" Frank asked quizzically.

"I am sure you will do very well without me."

"Not I," he declared fervently, his eyes sparkling. "Come with us, do. I dare swear you do not often have the chance to watch someone fence, and I know you are interested."

Alma was puzzled that his hostess had chosen not to accompany them and added his invitation to observe. When Diana turned to Mrs. Lewis and asked if she would like to see a fencing match, the old woman's face lit with enthusiasm and eventually all four headed for the Long Gallery.

Frank was an excellent fencer and conceived of this as an opportunity to exhibit one of his skills to Diana. The object of this exercise, however, was more interested in the general interaction between the two, explaining their advances, retreats, thrusts, and parries to Mrs. Lewis, who murmured admiringly the while.

"You see, Frank is beating in fourth, and feinting with a straight thrust, while Lord Alma parries with the fourth and Frank deceives and lunges. Well done."

Mrs. Lewis had not the faintest idea what all these

terms meant, but she was entranced by the spectacle all the same and urged Diana to keep up her commentary. Alma frequently allowed Frank to take the initiative but his defensive tactics were brilliant and Diana longed to fence with him, though she refused to suggest it again herself. If he wished to fence with her, an amateur, he would have to propose it himself. Perhaps he would become bored enough for even that.

The familiar pinched look began to appear on Alma's face after a lengthy exhibition and Diana feared he would not admit his fatigue. She watched for another ten minutes, becoming impatient with Frank for not realizing that his opponent was spent. Unobserved she rang and when a footman arrived in answer to the summons, she sent him off directly to have tea served in the main parlor and announced to the two that their bout must be concluded. Frank appeared reluctant to relinquish his sport, since he felt that he had showed to excellent advantage. Alma gladly lowered his foil and removed his mask; he refused to acknowledge his pain and exhaustion, but he had seldom greeted the announcement of tea with such alacrity.

Mrs. Lewis fluttered over the teapot with enthusiastic comments on the fencing skills of the young men. Frank was as susceptible to flattery as he was handy at delivering it, and repaid her enthusiasm by devoting some minutes in conversation with her. Alma took the opportunity to tell Diana that he would be retiring to his room to take care of some correspondence. "And I wish you will not allow that young man to ride Crusader," he muttered darkly.

"No," she replied thoughtfully, "I think you are right. I fear he would do some mischief."

Although Diana did not really want to be alone with Frank, she felt it was inevitable. He had entertained her guest for her and she owed him the drive he soon requested. His ornate phaeton was at the stables and she wrapped a shawl about her to accompany him there.

"I dare say you noticed how much better a fencer I am than your guest, Diana," he remarked as they settled themselves in the carriage.

"What I noticed, Frank, was that you did not call a halt to the bout when you could see that Lord Alma was flagging," she replied with asperity.

"And why should I?" he asked indignantly. "I wore him down."

"I believe I mentioned in my note that he had recently suffered an injury. You might have realized that he has not as yet recovered his strength."

"You refine too much on it, Diana," he said crossly. "Come now, it's a beautiful day. Let us forget all that and enjoy our drive."

They tooled along the lanes around the neighborhood while Frank disclosed to Diana his latest accomplishments in amateur dramatics, boxing, driving four-in-hand, gambling, and women. This last was only an inducement to her to understand how desirable he really was and what a bargain she would be passing up if she refused his renewed addresses to her. As they approached the Park again, but still out of sight of the stables, he stopped his pair and turned to her.

"Do say you will marry me, Diana. You cannot be interested in that clodhopper Dodge. What a dull life you would lead with him! Marry me and you will see some excitement." He attempted to kiss her but she pushed him away. Chagrined he said, "Do not be so prudish, Diana. If you would let me kiss you, you would understand how it could be with us." Convinced that this was true, he grasped her wrists and pinned them behind her so that he was able to bestow on her a passionate kiss. She bit him.

Her voice was cold and angry when he abruptly released her. "Drive me home this minute, Frank, or I will get out and walk the rest of the way. I do not wish to see you again."

Since it was incomprehensible to Frank that his advances should be repulsed, he was genuinely dumbfounded. When he did not urge the horses to motion immediately, Diana jumped down from the high phaeton and, ignoring the pain in her ankle she twisted as she struck the ground, stalked up the lane without a backward glance.

Alma, watching this episode from his window, decided that all the men in the neighborhood must be lunatics, and felt very little sympathy for Diana when she began to limp once Frank (in a snit) took himself off in the other direction.

While George Savile read a book at The Bush in Staines and the rain continued, and his sister stormed about her bedchamber in an excess of anger at Frank for attempting to kiss her, Lord Vallert arrived at Trafford Hall. Vallert was not an early riser, especially after an evening when he had entertained his friends—a bachelor celebration of his engagement, he had informed them. It was, therefore, late in the afternoon when he arrived at Trafford Hall, and he was shown into the Red Parlor by a footman who was not sure exactly whom he should inform of the arrival.

Although Lord Vallert had given him his card and asked for Miss Alonna Sanfield, the footman was aware that young ladies did not receive young gentlemen unattended. Since Lady Trafford was unavailable, he determined to find Lord Trafford, but he was unsuccessful and eventually a message was sent to Alonna that Lord Vallert awaited her in the Red Parlor.

Alonna was sitting with her sister when this intelligence was brought to her and her distressed countenance caused Margaret to exclaim, "What is it, love? Who is he?"

Owing to her sister's condition at the time of her arrival and the excitement which had followed, Alonna had pushed the episode of the engagement announcement to the back of her mind. She now took the opportunity to inform her sister of the precise reason she had come to Trafford Hall.

"So you do not wish to marry him?" Margaret asked quietly. "It is not just that he has been so foolish as to insert the announcement?"

"I call it more than foolish!" Alonna exclaimed. "It was stupid, unfeeling, thoughtless, and dishonest!"

"I see that you do *not* want to marry him," her sister laughed. "Well, I cannot say I blame you. I would not be put in such a position for the world. Did Papa promise to have the announcement repudiated?"

"Not precisely, but what else can he do?"

Margaret studied her sister through lowered eyelids. "Papa has changed since Mama's death, Alonna. I can tell from his letters. He wants to be free of his family, and you are the last one left. Do not let him force you into a disagreeable marriage. You can make your home here with me if there are any problems."

"He was not very helpful," Alonna admitted sadly. "I had hoped that by tomorrow I might receive a copy of the repudiation from him."

"I would not count on it, love. You had best go to Lord Vallert and see what he has to say. He has probably talked with Papa."

"How can I face him after what he has done? I don't want to be alone with him," she admitted softly.

"You will manage, my dear. The house is full of servants, some of whom will undoubtedly be listening at the keyhole."

Alonna smiled wistfully. "All right, I shall see him, but if I do not return to you within half an hour you must send me help." She marched out of the room with her chin held high.

Vallert had been left cooling his heels for some time before Alonna arrived at the door. He rose and bowed formally to her, then strode forward and attempted to take her hand. Refusing to allow this, she seated herself on a rather uncomfortable armchair upholstered in red plush which matched the red damask draperies in the room. Vallert seated himself opposite her in an identical chair and opened his mouth to speak.

Alonna imperiously waved him to silence. "The only thing I wish to hear from your lips, Lord Vallert, is that a retraction of our engagement announcement has been published." She tapped her fingertips on the arms of the chair and waited while he decided how to answer her.

"Now, Miss Sanfield," he said at length, "there is really no necessity for a retraction. If you consider your position for a moment you will see that a prompt wedding is the best solution to the whole matter."

"My position?" she asked coldly.

"Yes, your position, dear lady. Your father has sent me here to fetch you back to town. He is firm in his desire that you marry me, and since the engagement has been announced I feel it would be better if the matter were expedited."

"Do you?"

"Yes, indeed. You will feel more comfortable once we are husband and wife, and the little annoyance this has caused you will soon be forgotten," he said with a bland and confident smile.

"I wish to have you understand one thing, Lord Vallert. I shall never marry you. I told you so some days ago and you had the audacity to act in this underhanded way. If there was ever any possibility that I might have changed my mind, it no longer exists, and you may tell my father so," she added with an out thrust chin.

"But your father says you must marry me!"

"I doubt my father said any such thing," she asserted. His expression became mocking and she went on, "And even if he had, it would make no difference. He cannot force me to marry you. I shall come of age in a year and during that period of time I may remain with my sister if he does not wish to abide by my decision. That is all I have to say to you, Lord Vallert, except that if I do not have a copy of the retraction in my hands within the week I will take it upon myself to have one printed, and you can be sure that the manner in which I shall do so will not leave your reputation undamaged." Alonna rose from her chair and proceeded to the door, intent on ignoring his angry, red face and blustering words. The last thing she heard before closing the door behind her was. "You would not dare!"

Alonna sighed as she mounted the stairs to her sister's room. In her attempt to be firm she had merely aggravated the young man's hot temper further. Heaven knew what he would do now. Obviously she was far too inexperienced for such a man as George Savile; she could not even manage one obstreperous suitor.

chapter eight

Diana had been in no mood to encounter Lord Alma after her afternoon drive with Frank, and she was relieved that he took his meal in his room. His attendance in the music room would have been welcome, but she contented herself with the amusing thought that he was no doubt studying the plant life of Cambridgeshire in his room. Mrs. Lewis provided pleasant if unstimulating companionship and Diana found it wise to suggest an early retiring hour when her companion began to nod over her embroidery.

In the morning Jenkins assured his mistress that her project would be complete by midday. He still shook his head disapprovingly, but Diana was convinced that it was the only solution to Alma's entertainment. She did, however, send a message up to him inviting him to go fishing with her that morning, or alone if he preferred, for George's equipment would be put at his disposal.

When the message reached him Alma was dressed, and his mood had swung once more toward friendship with his "younger brother," so he joined Diana in the breakfast parlor where she was sipping at the last of her morning chocolate.

"Does fishing appeal to you?" she asked, looking up.

"Yes, I've always enjoyed it. You don't chatter while you're fishing, do you?"

"Never," she replied, her eyes twinkling.

"Good. Then let's go together."

She led him to her favorite spot along the river where the mossy bank was warmed by the sun the whole of the morning. Without the least embarrassment he spread the rug he had carried and lay down on it, offering her a pole as he did so. They stayed there companionably silent for several hours, occasionally exchanging languid, low-voiced remarks on the wildlife which wandered by, or compliments on each other's catch.

"Let's take ourselves off now and have our fish for luncheon," Diana suggested when the sun was overhead.

Alma agreed and asked as they packed away their supplies, "Did you think about more things to study?"

"No," she replied with a puzzled frown. "I did not really think much at all this morning. I just . . . felt good."

He smiled at her. "Is that something new?"

"Well, I seem to spend a lot of my time planning what I am to do next, thinking about what I will enjoy most, or I am doing something, you know, and then I am only thinking about that. Perhaps I don't spend enough time just sitting still and being happy."

"That's what I enjoy," he admitted, "and fishing is such a marvellous excuse for it." Alma was amused that she seemed truly surprised by her unprecedented behavior.

"Will you have luncheon with Mrs. Lewis and me today, so that she can thank you for the fish? I have warned the kitchen that we will be bringing some."

When he hesitated, she glanced at him imploringly. "I shall have a cushion placed on your chair."

"Oh, very well." He grimaced. "I feel sure Mrs. Lewis does not care a fig if I join the two of you for meals."

"Actually, I fear she forgets you for the most part, and when she remembers you she thinks you're rather odd."

"I cannot blame her. The poor woman looks at me so strangely when I do not sit down. You must not think I do not urge her to seat herself, either, Miss Savile, for I do."

"I know, but you have a title and she simply cannot bring herself to sit when you are standing, unless I am there to do so first." They had reached the house by this time and Diana handed the basket of fish to a footman to take to the kitchen. "They should be ready within twenty minutes. I will seek out Mrs. Lewis and a cushion."

When Alma joined the two ladies in the dining parlor precisely twenty minutes later, Mrs. Lewis was not able to hide her surprise at seeing him there, and he and Diana shared an amused glance. Diana waved him to the chair provided with a cushion and turned to Mrs. Lewis. "Lord Alma and I have spent the morning fishing, ma'am. Cook has prepared our catch for us."

"Oh, dear," Mrs. Lewis murmured, crestfallen. "It has been the bane of my life, Miss Diana, what with my husband a navy man and all, but I must confess I do not like to eat fish!"

Alma and Diana burst out laughing, much to the old woman's astonishment. Diana tried to placate her by saying, "It is just that I only induced Lord Alma to join us for luncheon so that you might thank him for the catch. Do not trouble yourself, Mrs. Lewis, my dear. I am sure Cook will send along enough cold meats and fruit to serve for you."

Mrs. Lewis looked slightly mollified by, if not totally comprehending of this explanation. After all, she saw no reason why Lord Alma should need any inducement to take his meals with his hostess. Seeing her continued reserve with him, Alma, seated awkwardly on the left half of his bottom, exerted himself to converse with her. She was soon cheerfully telling him of her husband's career and sad demise, of the years she had spent in Linton, and of the Saviles as children. In spite of the fact that Alma said very little during the meal, Mrs. Lewis retired to the small parlor with a much better opinion of him.

Diana could see that the strain of sitting had taken its toll and she allowed Alma to wander off when the meal was complete, but she left word to have him join her in the stables if he should ask for her. Her own impatience to see the completed project made her take a hasty leave of Mrs. Lewis.

A delighted smile spread over her face when she saw it. "It's perfect!" With small wheels and various pieces from an old dog cart, Jenkins and his assistants had assembled a sturdy carriage which one drove by standing between the wheels, on the order of a Roman-style chariot. One of the stable lads, Josh, had been the one to test this remarkable vehicle, and his enthusiasm was unbounded.

"Did people really drive like that, ma'am?" he asked.

"Well, certainly they raced with such chariots long ago. I cannot imagine that it would have provided a very comfortable means of transportation, but it may have for the sturdier of them. I really do not know much about chariots, though I have seen pictures of them. I shall have to read up on the subject."

Jenkins, well aware of Diana's curiosity about anything which caught her fancy, cast his eyes heavenward. "You do not think the young lord likely to break his neck in this contraption, Miss Diana?"

"I should think it unlikely, but if it does not please him, he need not drive it. And your efforts would still not be wasted," she added hastily, "for I could devise a play around it for next Christmastime."

"That I would like to see," he retorted.

"And so you shall, then," she replied pertly. "Come, Jenkins, are you not the least bit pleased with it?"

He broke into a slow smile. "That I am, Miss Diana, for I was not sure it could be done."

"I'm grateful to all of you. Could we mark his name on it?"

There was a general discussion of the best method of performing this task and eventually Diana agreed that she would simply draw ALMA on the largest piece of foolscap she could lay her hands on, in her very best copperplate hand and Jenkins would attach it to the chariot for her. When she returned in an hour this was done, and they were still admiring the sign when Alma himself appeared in the stable.

He looked at the chariot and then at Diana. "Is this my surprise?" he asked incredulously.

"Do you not like it?" She suddenly felt uncertain. "The Romans drove chariots standing up, you know, and I had thought it would provide a challenge for you." The excitement of a few moments before had turned to alarm. Perhaps he was angry for such a silly idea on her part. "There is no need for you to use it," she hurried on. "I have told Jenkins that we shall use it in a Christmas play if you do not wish to drive it."

"Don't be a goose!" he exclaimed, controlling an impulse to hug her in front of the whole stable staff. "How ever did you think of such a thing? No, don't tell me," he laughed. "I can imagine."

Diana felt relief flood through her. "We've put your name on it, and Jenkins thinks Charger would be best to pull it. Josh has used it with him and found everything secure. Would you like to try it now? Jenkins is afraid you'll break your neck, but I really don't think so," she said seriously, her eyes dancing.

"If I do, you are not to hold yourself to blame," he retorted.

"No more shall I."

There was a great deal of excitement surrounding the harnessing of the horse to the chariot and Alma's testing its balance. The entire complement of the stable staff provided a cheer as he asked them to release the horse. It was an entirely unique experience for him to drive in such a manner, of course, requiring a great deal of balance and a different touch on the reins altogether. He had to break himself of the desire to use the ribbons as a balancing mechanism, for that confused the horse and tended to slow him. The exhilaration which encompassed Alma as he urged the horse to still greater speed did not tempt him to release his caution, however. For an hour he tooled along the lanes near the Park, laughing at the astonished faces of the people who passed him.

When he brought the chariot back to the stables he found it was more difficult to alight than to drive the thing, but the stable lads ran to his assistance. "Tomorrow," he informed them, "I should like to drive two horses tandem. Then I will race Miss Savile." He turned to bestow a radiant smile on her. "Will you accept my challenge, ma'am?"

"Certainly," she responded readily. "Was it fun?"

"Yes. A bit awkward at first, almost more like riding

than driving in some ways. You feel very much closer to the horse than in a carriage, and more dependent on your own ability. I'm sorry, I didn't offer you a chance to try it. Would you like to?"

"Perhaps another time. I must join Mrs. Lewis for tea now. Do you come?"

"Yes, I could stand a cup, and I will even sit down so that Mrs. Lewis will not be uncomfortable," he offered handsomely.

"There is no need, for you charmed her at lunch," Diana laughed. "I cannot doubt but that she will even accept your standing now."

They began to walk toward the house and Alma suddenly placed his hand on her arm. "I cannot express to you how grateful I am, Miss Savile. It was a very clever idea and I feel better just knowing there is something I can *do*. Oh, I have enjoyed the archery and the fencing and the fishing, but not being able to ride or drive was a nuisance. Worse than a nuisance. It put me in a very black temper and I could not feel easy. I . . . well, thank you."

"I'm pleased that it will serve," she responded happily as he removed his hand from her arm and they continued toward the house. "Do you think the chariot goes faster than a phaeton?"

"It is lighter, of course, and everything would indicate that it should. We shall see. You will not mind losing, I trust," he said quizzingly.

"Not I. I have spent most of my life losing races to George. He was never one to let me win out of softheartedness. I feel sure you will be the same," she laughed.

"'Depend on it," he retorted as they entered the small parlor.

During their absence Mrs. Lewis had sustained a visit from a friend just back from London. "She has brought me several papers from town, Miss Diana. You may wish to see them."

Diana thanked her for the offer and did avail herself of them after the tea tray had been removed and Mrs.

Lewis had begun once more on her embroidery. "Oh, dear," she said pathetically. "He was too late. Poor George."

Pacing about the room, ready to excuse himself, Alma looked at her questioningly. Her stricken expression startled him.

"There is an announcement of the engagement of Miss Alonna Sanfield to Lord Vallert," she explained sadly, biting her lip. Diana lapsed into thought for a while, unaware of the concern she was causing her companions. "I think I must go to London."

"To London?" Mrs. Lewis asked quaveringly. "I thought you did not even like to go to town, Miss Diana."

"No, I do not really care for it, but I think George must be feeling rather down and he could use my company." Her eyes chanced to land on Alma at that moment and his ludicrous expression drew her up sharply. "No, of course I cannot go now. What am I thinking of? Forgive me, Lord Alma. If George needs company he will surely return to the Park," she prophesied with an overly brilliant smile.

Alma was at a pass. Miss Savile obviously longed to go to her brother but felt she must stay to entertain him, and he could not suggest that she go because that would leave him without either host or hostess at the Park, and he could not leave yet. Well, he could manage without a host or hostess for a few days, he supposed. She had been very kind to him, attentive to his needs and sympathetic to his moodiness. "If you wish to go to London, Miss Savile, I hope you will not allow me to detain you. I can manage here on my own."

Diana studied her hands and bit her lip. "No, there is no need for me to go. The paper is three days old now, and George has not returned. He was not altogether sure . . . well, I shall just assume he is fine," she said stoutly.

Mrs. Lewis surveyed the two young people uneasily. That Mr. Savile would be affected by the announcement of this young lady's engagement, she surmised readily enough, but she did not like to see Miss Diana so downcast, so she said heartily, "If you were to go to London you would probably pass Mr. Savile on the road, my dear. If he has decided to come home, that is."

Diana met the old woman's concerned gaze. "Yes, it would be very foolish of me to rush off in such a helter-skelter fashion, would it not, Mrs. Lewis? I shall stay right where I am and wait for word from him."

It had not occurred to George to send word to his sister. He had decided the previous day, whenever his concentration drifted from his book, that if the rain had not stopped by the next morning he would hire a closed carriage to take him to Lymington. He was in luck, however, and a watery sun shone through that following day, so he set out through the mud regardless of the tales of flooding. The whole day was spent fording unknown and unexpected streams across the roads, being splattered with mud each time he passed another carriage and urging each new pair of horses to face the inconveniences with courage. George reached the Old Toll House at Lymington late in the evening—cold, wet and muddy. The meal he ordered in his room was nourishing if not very appetizing looking, and the brandy seemed heaven-sent.

George was tempted to discard his distressed clothing forever, but instead decided to pay a premium for having it respectably cleaned by a maid who tutted the while she examined it. He had not brought more than a few changes of clothing, and he had no intention of presenting himself at Franston Hall other than respectably dressed. He had begun to question the wisdom of his journey, but it bore in on him the fact that he was more deeply attached to Alonna than even he had previously suspected. Though he realized that there was little hope of a successful conclusion, he looked forward to the next day with a great deal of tension which was wholly foreign to his placid nature.

Lord Vallert had returned to London in high dudgeon, and the interview he conducted with Lord Franston did not please either of them. Alonna's father refused to order his daughter back to London or to retrieve her. He simply said, "She'll come about, young man. Give her time. No need to take on so."

Vallert lost his temper then. "Why the hell shouldn't I take on? The chit said if I did not have a retraction printed she would do so herself, and threatened to blacken my character in the process! Have you no control over your daughter?"

Lord Franston eyed him malevolently. "Obviously no more than you have over your intended, you young gudgeon. Retract the announcement. You can insert it again when Alonna has agreed and it will appear merely a lover's quarrel. The *ton* will lap it up, slap me if they won't."

"I will appear a fool!"

"And so you are, for inserting the announcement in the first place without receiving my daughter's permission."

"Do you think she would actually have the retraction printed herself in such a way as to cast a bad light on me?" Vallert demanded.

"Couldn't say. Don't know her very well, you see. Spent most of her time the last few years in the country."

"I shall not print a retraction," Vallert asserted hotly. "I intend to marry your daughter!"

The older man regarded him thoughtfully. "I cannot see why you wish to marry a young woman who doesn't want you but I wash my hands of the matter. You will no doubt find out in time if she meant what she said. My own guess, for what it's worth, is that she did. She has but a year before her majority and I imagine her sister will be willing to house her until then. I cannot force her to marry you. You'd be smart to cut your losses."

Vallert stalked out without another word, leaving Lord Franston to mutter about ill-mannered young puppies to a nonexistent audience. Alonna's father had the uneasy feeling that he had not handled the entire matter as he ought, but he had no ambition to involve himself further. Let Margaret take his daughter off his hands; as far as he was concerned it was almost as good as marrying her off.

chapter nine

Diana awoke the next morning with a heavy heart. George was the person she loved most in the whole world and she ached for his disappointment. In all the years they had talked together as contemporaries (and he had treated her as such for the last ten years), he had never before spoken of any woman as being someone he desired to marry; and he had led an active social life in London from the time he first went there at twenty, when she was only eight. In those days, their parents already dead, he had provided her with a kindly governess and frequently stayed at the Park for long periods of time. All those years he had met young women daily at his home and in town, and never once had he mentioned one he wanted to marry.

It might be, she thought, that he had decided it was time to marry and had chosen the best of those available, but she thought not. He had spoken with real warmth about this Alonna Sanfield, had even thought of asking Diana to come to London to meet her. Even though he had appeared to question the choice of such a young and inexperienced woman, she knew that he had already decided to try his luck. How frustrating not even to have a chance, to be so close and lose her without ever knowing if she would have had him.

Diana drew herself up abruptly. George had left her with a responsibility and that was the only thing she could do for him now—make sure that Lord Alma was kept occupied and reasonably happy. She was determined to do that one small thing for her brother. Perhaps even now George was headed for the Park, as Mrs. Lewis had suggested. She sighed and rose from her bed to dress for the morning.

Alma had joined them the previous evening for dinner and several games of three-handed whist. He did not come to breakfast but met Diana in the hall shortly after she left Mrs. Lewis in the small parlor.

"Shall we have our race now?" he asked cheerfully.

"Yes, but you will want to practice with the horses tandem first. I have to speak with the housekeeper, but I will join you at the stables in half an hour, if that's agreeable."

When she joined him there, the grooms were ready to harness the horses to her own phaeton. George had presented it to her on her birthday almost a year ago. "Have you marked out a course?" she asked Alma.

"We have a marker there beyond the gate for the start and finish. Twice around the south field. Is that satisfactory?"

"Perfectly. How do the horses handle in tandem with the chariot?"

"A trifle sticky, but I think I'm getting the knack of it."

"Good. Do you wish to make a wager on the race? George always does."

"What sort of wager?"

"When we were young we did it for chores and errands, now we wager fantastic amounts of money—imaginary, of course."

Alma could not offhand think of any ridiculous bet to make, though an absurd idea popped into his mind to be immediately discarded. "What do you say to a guinea?"

"You're on."

The grooms held their horses at the starting line until Jenkins gave the signal to start. Diana took an immediate lead because Alma was having trouble controlling his horses. The path was wide enough for the two vehicles side by side, but Diana maintained a full length ahead of Alma the first time around the south field. When they were halfway around the second time he began to gain on her, accustomed now to the speed and the movement of the chariot. As they came past the field and onto the stretch toward the stables his chariot wheel sank briefly into a hole which threw him slightly off balance. In his effort to maintain his stance his pressure on the reins caused the horses to swerve just enough to throw the chariot wheel against that of the phaeton.

Diana had given herself up to the excitement of the race and was taken completely unawares by the light blow to her wheel. The phaeton tipped slightly and she was pitched out onto the grassy bank like a discarded container. George's words came back to her in a flash, 'Release the reins immediately if you are thrown,' and she did so. The breath was knocked out of her but her landing was no more disastrous than any of the falls she had taken as a child.

Such an enormous consequence to the light touching of wheels surprised Alma, but he cursed himself for a fool and drew in his horses ruthlessly. The woman was as light as a feather to fly off like that! He left the grooms starting toward them to cope with the phaeton and the chariot and raced back to his hostess.

By the time he reached her, Diana was sitting up and Alma, white with fear, stopped abruptly in front of her and gasped, "Are you all right? Dear God, I'm sorry, Diana. I tried to recover my balance. Are you hurt?"

"No, I don't think so. Just a little dazed." She held out her hand for him to help her up and he grasped it firmly to pull her to her feet, all the while looking for signs of an injury. Aware of his concern, Diana scolded, "Don't be so solicitous. There is nothing the matter with me."

"You're sure? Can you walk?"

She took several steps to prove that she could, bent and unbent her arms and wagged her head back and forth. "You see? Quite whole and undamaged."

"It's no joking matter," he retorted, still upset. "If you were not so small you would not have been flung out like that."

She laughed at him. "Well, you can hardly blame me for being small, Alma. I trust no harm came to the horses."

"I doubt they even realized you were thrown," he responded exasperatedly. The absurdity of their argument occurred to him then and they stood on the lane laughing until Jenkins arrived to reprove them for their behavior.

Diana adopted a mock solemnity immediately. "I am perfectly all right, Jenkins, and if the horses are likewise there is no need for any further remonstrances. Alma touched against my wheel and has been scolding me for being so small as to fly out of the carriage." She could not repress a gurgle of laughter, and the groom shook his head indulgently.

"Just so long as you're all right, Miss Diana," he grumbled and trudged off toward the stables.

"I think we are even now," Alma said, gazing down at her amused eyes.

"Not precisely," she said impishly, "but close enough."

"Careful, you wretched girl. You will make me blush," he rejoined as they started to walk down the lane. "You seem well accustomed to taking spills."

"I have had any number of them. George was wont to call me Disaster Diana when I was a child, but he dropped it when I actually hurt myself one time. That hardly makes sense, does it?"

"It makes perfect sense, Diana. I wonder, though, that George taught you so many sports if you were continually being tossed about by every light breeze."

Diana indignantly drew herself up to her fullest height. "I will have you know that I am the accredited woman archer of the area," she proclaimed haughtily.

"Then I can only suppose that you intended to shoot me," he rejoined, laughing.

"Mock me if you will, Alma. I am proud of being able to ride and drive and shoot a bow and arrow and fence and fish, and play billiards and dance and shoot a gun. I am grateful to George for teaching me."

"So am I," he admitted with a rueful grin. "And for letting you read about road surfacing and birds and plants and chariots."

"Actually, I haven't read much about chariots," she said thoughtfully, forgetting to be on her dignity. "Josh asked me if the Romans used them for transportation and

I could not be sure. I only know that they used them for racing."

"You will have to read up on it," he suggested, his eyes merry.

"Perhaps I shall."

Before heading for the house they checked at the stables to be sure that no harm had come to the horses. Reassured on that score Alma proposed a quiet game of billiards, since their race had ended so abruptly. He had nothing to complain of in George's pupil.

George left the inn in Lymington early that morning and set off for Franston Hall with only a further ten miles to cover. His driving coat with its several capes was acceptable if not immaculate, and he arrived at Franston Hall with rising spirits. These had time to diminish as the minutes lengthened before there was an answer at the door.

The elderly butler who eventually responded to his summons assured him that the family was away from home.

George offered his card and asked if Miss Alonna Franston was expected there. He thought perhaps the rain had delayed her as well as himself and that he might have arrived before her, though with a day's start it was highly unlikely.

"No, sir, we have had no word of her impending arrival. She and her father should be in London for the season."

A comic look of dismay stole over George's face. He had spent better than two days on a wild goose chase. "She has left London," he explained to the patient butler, "and I had thought she might be coming here."

The butler took pity on him. "Her sister near Colchester is expecting a child soon, sir. It may be that she has gone to her."

George's spirits lifted. "Near Colchester, you say?" He felt ludicrously grateful to the old man in spite of the fact that Colchester must be a good forty miles on the other side of London.

"Yes, sir, Trafford Hall it is."

"I thank you." George expressed his gratitude financially as well as in words and immediately took himself off. Without further delay, he started back for London, but did not arrive at his house until late at night, exhausted, and beginning to think better of his unprecedented impetuous behavior.

Allison and Walter Dodge arrived at the Park before Diana and her companions had finished luncheon. They were invited to partake of the meal and gladly accepted.

As she was seating herself, Allison explained, "We have been riding about the neighborhood all morning trying to dredge up every available person to come to dinner tonight. Mama has just heard from Aunt Louisa that she is arriving with her son and daughter this afternoon on their way to London."

This explanation clarified all for Diana but meant nothing to Mrs. Lewis or Alma, so she turned to them to expand on her friend's words. "Allison and Walter's Aunt Louisa is the Countess of Langley and she expects to be entertained like royalty whenever she chooses to arrive at someone's house. Mrs. Dodge usually has more notice, though," she frowned. "Are they only spending the one night, Allison?"

"So we believe. The message was intolerably brief," her friend remarked dryly. "Will you come? Mrs. Lewis and Lord Alma, too, of course. There will be dancing after."

Mrs. Lewis had not had such an opportunity in years and beamed her pleasure at the idea. Lord Alma looked skeptical but asked, "Is her son Carson Barsett?"

Walter spoke for the first time. "Yes, do you know him?"

"I've met him several times in London. A very good fellow."

Then you will come?" Allison asked pleadingly.

When Alma continued to hesitate, Diana said, "If you will place an inconspicuous cushion on his dining chair, I am sure he can be convinced." She smiled pertly at her guest, who raised an eyebrow in mock censure.

"I should be delighted," he replied.

Allison giggled and said she would see to it personally. The brother and sister then rose to take their leave, since they had two more calls to make and still be at their home to receive their honored guests. "And, Diana," Allison said, "Mama said I must especially tell you to look your best."

With a slight flush Diana murmured, "You may assure her that I shall do so, Allison." Her friend nodded and left.

Alma had overheard this interchange and considered it either extremely rude or highly mysterious. Since he found it difficult to imagine Allison Dodge deliberately being rude to her older friend, he decided that the customs prevailing in Cambridgeshire must be very different from those in his native Northampton.

During the afternoon Diana left Alma to his own devices, as she had much to do if she were to obey Mrs. Dodge's instruction. George had several times brought her gowns from London, and she must look one out and have it ready to wear. She chose a striped poplin with a quilted petticoat in shades of blue and white. George had brought her long gloves of the same shade of blue which would reach to the elbow where the dress sleeve extended. It was necessary to look out matching slippers and reticule, as well as the ivory fan she kept for special occasions. The butler was instructed to retrieve the diamond necklace, diadem and earring set she had inherited from her mother. Her hair style was the most difficult change.

For the last five years Diana had purposely played down her looks. On special occasions such as this she obediently rigged herself out in the height of fashion, but she had learned that she did not really wish to attract the kind of attention she received when she dressed stylishly. Not that there was anything wrong with her daily outfits. They were acceptable garments in themselves, but were never fitted to her figure. Being small it was easy to allow for some growth, which would never take place now that she was almost three-and-twenty. Her usual hair style was a severe drawing back of her hair, tied with a ribbon. She always looked neat and clean—and uninspired. That was precisely what she wished.

George had discouraged this deliberate game of hers. He understood the reasons for it and sympathized with her but could not like it. However, there were few times when George was insistent with Diana about anything, and though he continued a gentle prodding at her about her attire, and brought her fashionable garments from London, he allowed her to go her own way.

Her maid's assistance was necessary to achieve a decent hair style. Diana chose to have it combed up in back with a profusion of locks clustered about her face and a ringlet pulled down to rest on her left shoulder. The brown hair glowed from the brushing and made an enchanting frame for her face. Diana made an annoyed smirk at herself in the mirror; the hair style was very flattering. Her maid set the diadem carefully amidst the locks, its diamonds sparkling wildly in the late afternoon sunlight. Diana sighed.

When it was time to join Mrs. Lewis and Alma in the parlor she walked there nervously toying with her fan. A footman leaped to open the door for her and, with the memory of George's instructions on elegance running through her head, drifted regally into the room. Mrs. Lewis turned to smile cheerfully at her and exclaimed, "My, how lovely you look, Miss Diana." Alma stood, stunned. When Diana curtsied to him, murmuring, "Lord Alma," he managed a bow with a startled, "Miss Savile." They had drifted during the day into calling each other more familiarly, but the formality of the evening made a decided change.

Diana spoke with Mrs. Lewis for a few moments to assure her anxious friend that the gown she had brought from her cottage was charming and very appropriate for the evening. "You will find the Countess very stuffy no doubt, Mrs. Lewis, but do not let her put you out of countenance. She will try; she does with everyone she meets."

"Oh," Mrs. Lewis sighed with fallen hopes. "I dare say I shall not be able to say a word to her then. Anyone who wishes to is able to put me out of countenance."

Diana gave a gurgle of laughter. "Well, I shall protect you from the dragon then, and Lord Alma will, won't you, sir?"

Only vaguely aware of their discussion, Alma immediately agreed. He had decided that it was not Diana's suitors who were lunatics, but she herself. If she possessed such stunning beauty she should not be hiding behind a dowdy hair style and uninteresting clothes. Dressed modishly she was a perfect miniature, delicately exquisite, almost fragile. He could think of nothing to say to her and found himself unaccountably awkward with her.

Taking no notice of his silence as they drove to the Dodges', she spent the time attempting to put Mrs. Lewis at ease by regaling her with anecdotes of the Countess's previous visits to the neighborhood. When they arrived and Lord Alma had been introduced to Mr. and Mrs. Dodge, the latter took Diana aside and nodded approvingly. "Thank you, my dear. I know it is never your wish, but I find Louisa rather intimidating on these visits and you always put me in heart."

"Dear ma'am, it is no trouble for me, and George would be delighted." Diana grinned at her hostess. "Does Mr. Dodge's sister stay only the one night?"

"So she says. I am always pleased to see my niece and nephew and wish they would stay longer, but . . ."

"I understand perfectly, ma'am. Shall I introduce my companions to the Countess? You have more guests arriving."

"Thank you, Diana, I should appreciate it."

Diana beckoned to Mrs. Lewis and Lord Alma and approached the Countess of Langley without the least hesitation. Having met the woman on a dozen occasions, she was not a bit in awe of her. Allison was standing behind her aunt's chair and said, "You will remember Miss Savile, Aunt Louisa."

"Certainly I remember her," the Countess replied, her sharp eyes regarding Diana suspiciously. "I see you are in your usual looks, Miss Savile. I cannot imagine what is wrong with the young men hereabouts that you are not wed yet, at your age."

"It is a mystery to me, my lady," Diana replied, her mouth twitching. "May I present my friend Mrs. Lewis, who is a resident of Linton?"

The countess did not take a moment to survey the old woman's outmoded gown and remarked, "So I should suppose. How do you do, Mrs. Lewis?"

Mrs. Lewis curtsied slightly and murmured something unintelligible. Diana turned to Lord Alma and he stepped forward, elegant in his formal attire. "Lord Alma is a friend of my brother's, Lady Langley. He is acquainted with your son."

The countess raked Alma with piercing eyes. "Indeed. How do you do, Lord Alma?"

Alma bowed and replied politely, making some remark about having met Carson in London on several occasions. The countess appeared unimpressed with this knowledge but would have questioned him further had not Mrs. Dodge arrived to present other guests, and Diana was able to remove her guests from the lady's presence.

When Diana had led Mrs. Lewis to a chair near Lady Edwards, and the two women had fallen into animated conversation, she took Alma across the room to where Walter stood with his cousins. Jenette remembered her from previous visits and her brother obviously did also. He clasped her hand firmly and murmured, "A pleasure, Miss Savile. It is too long between our meetings. Do you never come to London?"

"Very seldom, my lord. I believe you are acquainted with Lord Alma?" she asked, indicating her companion. While the two men acknowledged each other and discussed mutual friends, Diana took the opportunity to escape and greet her neighborhood friends as they arrived. She was soon the center of a group of young men and felt thankful when dinner was announced, only to find herself seated between Frank Edwards and Carson Barsett, both of whom were intent on attracting her attention.

During the soup she spoke politely with Frank, shifting her head toward Carson for the ragout of breast of veal. Frank once again claimed her while she picked at the boiled leg of lamb with cauliflower. Diana refused the side dishes of jugged hare and marrow pudding but accepted a serving of roast pig at Carson's urging. The second course consisted largely of fish and game, with apricot fritters and almond cheesecakes. Diana's appetite, never large, deserted her long before her neighbors had completed their repast. Her neck had begun to ache from switching constantly back and forth between them and she gratefully followed Mrs. Dodge when the women retired.

Lady Langley beckoned to her when they returned to the parlor and Diana obediently went to sit near her. "Is that young man one of your suitors?"

"Which young man, Lady Langley?" Diana asked, confused.

"Lord Alma, the one you introduced to me," the older woman grunted.

"No, ma'am. He is a friend of my brother's and is staying at the Park while he recovers from an accident."

"He looks healthy enough to me," Lady Langley proclaimed.

"I dare say," Diana said coolly. "Nonetheless, he is recovering from an accident."

"Is your brother at the Park now?"

"No, Mrs. Lewis is staying with me, Lady Langley. Does Jenette have her come-out this season?"

"Yes, and I have high hopes for her," the countess declared vigorously.

"She is a charming young woman and I hope she will enjoy her season. No doubt she and Allison will see a deal of each other. I imagine it must be bewildering for a young woman to have no friends about when she arrives in London."

"You never had a season, did you?" demanded the countess. "Why did not your brother see to it?"

Diana did not reply to these questions, as she considered them none of Lady Langley's business. Instead she asked Lady Langley of her husband's health.

The Countess, aware that Miss Savile never allowed herself to be bullied, replied suitably as to the Earl's constitution and vaguely dismissed the younger woman.

Diana joined Mrs. Lewis and Lady Edwards across the room for a while before seating herself with Allison and Jenette.

"Was Mama quizzing you?" Jenette asked uncomfortably.

"We discussed your coming season," Diana replied easily. "I was thinking that you and Allison are fortunate to be having your come-outs at the same time."

"Yes, I think so," Jenette confessed. She and Allison began to discuss the arrangements for their balls and Diana took the opportunity to relax in their company without being drawn into their conversation.

When the men rejoined the ladies there was a general move toward the card tables for the older people and the ballroom for the younger ones. Diana was besieged with requests from Walter, Frank and Carson, as well as a number of the other young men from the area. Lord Alma did not approach her until later in the evening, after he had danced with Allison and Jenette and Carol Edwards.

"Have you the next dance free, Miss Savile?" he asked stiffly.

"Not this one, Lord Alma, but the succeeding one," she replied.

"I hope you will save it for me."

"I shall."

When he led her into the country dance he studied her carefully, as he had frequently during the evening. Her self-possession and fragility were at complete variance with the young woman, the "younger brother," he had been associating with for the better part of a week. There was no flirtatiousness in her even now, he thought grudgingly. The men buzzed about her like bees around a flower, their admiration continually proclaimed, and she accepted their acclamation with a distant politeness. Alma had watched her draw out the shyest of the young men and keep at arm's length the most ardent, Frank Edwards.

"Have you told Walter of your chariot, Lord Alma?" Diana asked.

"Yes. He has offered to race me tomorrow."

"That should be a good match. His bays are excellent and he drives well."

When he did not reply, she looked at him quizzingly and said, "And he will not fly out of his phaeton should you bump him."

Unable to respond to the levity of this sally, Alma continued to regard her with an impassive face and a disconcerted mind. The movement of the dance separated them and when they were rejoined Diana remarked lightly, "It will be all right tomorrow. Well, perhaps the next day, really." Again there was no response from him and she told him, when they were together, of the other people about them.

Diana was relieved when the dance ended and he left her abruptly at the side of the dance floor to be immediately claimed by Carson Barsett. Alma did not approach her again during the evening and was silent in the carriage as they returned to the Park, but Mrs. Lewis more than made up for his silence with her cheerful comments on the evening.

chapter ten

George Savile slept late the morning after he returned to London. When he had dressed, to the accompaniment of Stephen's aspersions on the condition of the clothes he returned with, he went once again to Lord Franston's town house. He was advised by the butler that Miss Sanfield had not returned to town and that her father was not at home.

"Do you know where I might find Lord Franston?"

"No, sir, I do not," the butler replied coldly.

"I understand Miss Sanfield is with her sister near Colchester," George ventured.

"I would not be at liberty to say, sir."

George sighed and left Berkeley Square no wiser. It was time he sought out Cranmer to see if his friend had any information on the situation. He should have done so before he left for Lymington, he thought ruefully, for his friend was perhaps one of the most well-informed men in London.

Cranmer, still in his dressing gown, obligingly invited George to join him at his breakfast. "Just arrive in town?" he asked as he devoured a morsel of sirloin.

"For the second time," George remarked with self-mockery.

Cranmer eyed him with amusement. "How so, George?"

"The first time I arrived I read of Miss Sanfield's engagement. I left town for several days after that. What do you know of it, Cranmer?"

"There is something strange about it," his friend mused. "Vallert is at great pains to explain her absence at such a time—went to her sister who was about to be confined. Franston says nothing, literally nothing. I ran into him last night, made some comment on it and he snubbed me." Cranmer laughed reminiscently. "Odd, I call that. I've heard it said that they've had a lover's quarrel, Miss Sanfield and Vallert. Very romantic, but I cannot believe it for a minute. Either her father is pressing her to marry him or . . . well, I really don't know, George. Think you should talk to the girl."

"I have been trying to," George admitted with a crooked grin. "Unfortunately, I assumed she had gone home when she left town, since no one seemed to know."

"You went to Lymington?" his friend asked incredulously.

George nodded. "Wet trip, too, Cranmer. I'm too old for all this nonsense."

"Her sister lives near Colchester."

"So I understand," George drawled.

"Married Trafford some years ago. Pretty girl."

"I agree."

"It's only four hours to Colchester."

"It will probably rain."

"I hear she just had twins."

"Indeed."

"Probably a good thing her sister went to her."

"No doubt."

"I imagine Miss Sanfield will not soon return to London."

"Oh, give over, Cranmer. I think I will return to the Park. I left Ellis there wounded."

"Really?"

"Yes, my sister accidentally shot him with an arrow."

Cranmer's eyes widened unbelievingly. "You're joking."

"Swear to God," George replied pleasantly.

"I cannot imagine Ellis liked that."

George rose to leave. "No, he was rather annoyed. Ask him to tell you about it one day."

"I will."

Diana also rose late that morning. She sat before the mirror and vigorously brushed out the curls and ringlets as best she could, catching her long hair at the nape of her neck with a green ribbon. Her finery of the evening before had all disappeared from sight, the jewels back to the butler's safekeeping and the gown stowed away by her maid. Only the ivory fan and reticule lay on the dressing table, to be whisked into a drawer by their owner. She donned the same gray dress she had worn two days previously and contemplated the tedious day she had in store for her. After such an event as the previous evening there was always a stream of young men calling to pay their compliments.

Dining alone in the breakfast parlor, she was informed that Mrs. Lewis had preceded her by an hour and that Lord Alma had taken his meal in his room. When she had nearly completed her meal she heard the sound of hoofbeats and glanced out the window to see Frank Edwards approaching the house. She sighed and rose to instruct the butler that Mr. Edwards was to be denied.

Mrs. Lewis welcomed her to the small parlor where she was already at work on a new seat cover. "Such an evening as we had. Did you enjoy yourself, Miss Diana?"

"Yes, it was very pleasant," Diana replied. She tried to share in her companion's enthusiasm for a half hour before the butler came to inform her that the Dodges and their cousins had arrived. "You may show them in, Jackson. And please send word to Lord Alma that they have arrived." As the butler was about to withdraw, Diana called after him, "Jackson, you had best tell Cook that there will likely be a number of extra people for luncheon."

The small parlor was soon crowded with the new arrivals, followed shortly by more. Lord Alma put in an appearance and pursed his mouth at the congregation. Approaching him hesitantly, Diana asked, "Would you mind if we used your race with Walter to clear everyone out of the house and down to the stables?"

"An excellent idea, Miss Savile," he replied tartly. "Does this happen every time you spend an evening out?"

Diana ignored the sarcasm in his voice and said evenly, "Yes, Lord Alma, it does." She turned then to the rest of her guests to announce that Walter and Lord Alma were about to conduct a race and everyone was welcome to view the spectacle. Although she stayed behind a moment to urge Mrs. Lewis to join them, the old woman had had enough excitement for a while and confessed that she would be happier sitting in the parlor with her embroidery. "I cannot say I blame you, ma'am," Diana admitted as she left to join the others.

The chariot received a variety of comments and had to be tested by each of the young men before the race was begun. There were a number of wagers made before the signal was given; the race was conducted over the same course as the previous day. This time Alma did not lag at the start but swung ahead of Walter immediately. Walter's bays quickly regained some of the distance and the vehicles went around the south field twice, practically neck and neck. In the final stretch, however, Alma's lighter carriage told and he drew ahead to win the race. He was flushed and in good spirits afterwards and offered the other men a chance to try the chariot. Diana ordered luncheon to be served at the edge of the wood near the stables.

Walter tried his own horses in the chariot, and then challenged Carson to a race with Carson driving Walter's phaeton. Again wagers were made, and again the chariot won. After the Barsetts left, the afternoon was spent matching horses and chariot and phaeton. The young women drifted off to the archery range for a while but returned to see the concluding race, where Alma in the chariot again won his race against Walter in his phaeton. The rest of the visitors began to leave then, and soon Diana and Alma were left alone at the stables to walk back to the house.

"A very pleasant afternoon, don't you agree?" she asked her companion cheerfully.

"Yes."

"Did the chariot win all of the races?"

"No, some young twig botched it once."

"That must have been when we were on the archery range."

"It was."

"Perhaps it would be more fair, then, to race the chariot with one horse against a phaeton with a pair," she suggested.

"Perhaps." Alma shoved his hands into his pockets.

Diana stopped walking and he hesitated. "We were friends yesterday," she said accusingly.

He made an impatient gesture with one hand. "The books came from Stillings this morning, Miss Savile."

"Did they? I am so glad you remembered," she replied wistfully.

"He started to walk again and she reluctantly accompanied him. "Are you still interested in studying the period?" he asked.

"Oh, yes. There are several churches in the area that have tombs like Nick's, and it pleases me to think of people in those times living right here where we do now."

Alma made no further comment. They reached the house and he bowed formally to Diana and went to his room. She joined Mrs. Lewis in the parlor but after a while went to speak with the cook. Diana had finally had enough of Alma's moods and tempers. When he did not present himself for dinner, she sent a message with his man that he would eat in the dining parlor with her and Mrs. Lewis, or not at all.

His lordship received this message with astonishment. He had rested after the exercise of the afternoon and had expected a tray to be sent to his room when he requested it. The little chit was treating him like a recalcitrant school boy, he stormed (though there was no one to hear him, since his valet had left to take his own meal in the housekeeper's room). Well, he wouldn't eat then, he thought sulkily. His stomach rumbled reprovingly. Eventually he presented himself in the dining parlor and made pleasant conversation with Mrs. Lewis. Diana he ignored completely. When the women withdrew he sat in solitary state and determined to drink George's cellars dry.

When George arrived his friend was still seated in the dining parlor, now well inebriated and aching abominably for having sat so long. George was advised of his friend's whereabouts and peered around the door but did not disturb him. He went instead to greet his sister and her companion. After a few minutes Mrs. Lewis discreetly excused herself, and Diana burst out immediately, "Oh, George, we have read of Miss Sanfield's engagement. I am so sorry."

"We will discuss that later, Diana. Right now I want to know why Ellis is sitting drunk in the dining parlor."

"Is he? I have not seen him since dinner," she replied crossly.

"I cannot believe that you have managed to stay at outs with him for a week, Diana," he said mildly.

"Well, and I have not, George. I have done everything in my power to entertain your friend. And after the first few days we were getting along splendidly . . . until last night."

"What happened last night?"

"Mrs. Dodge entertained the Countess," Diana offered by way of explanation.

"I see. You dressed for the occasion?"

"Yes, she especially asked that I should, George, and ever since Alma has not spoken to me above what is absolutely necessary."

"I cannot see that he should be drinking himself into oblivion if that is all."

"Well, you see, George, I grew tired of his ups and downs, his black moods and then lightheartedness. I refused to have a tray sent up to him for dinner."

George surveyed her exasperatedly. "That is not like you, Diana."

She lifted her chin and there was a suspicion of a tear in her eye. "I don't care, George. I find it intolerable to be treated one day as a friend and the next with odious formality. I have racked my brain for ways to entertain him. I have spent nearly a week catering to his starts and stops. I had had enough. *You* may look after him now; I wash my hands of him."

"All right, I will speak with him. Go to bed, love," he said gently.

"She nodded and left the room. George watched her

retreating form uneasily, then he went to the dining parlor. He took a seat beside Alma, who gazed at him owlishly and asked, "When did you get here, George?"

"A few minutes ago, Ellis. Why are you sitting here? You cannot be comfortable."

"No," Alma admitted, surprised. "Not at all comfortable. Damned awkward, this wound," he growled malevolently.

"No doubt," George replied dampeningly. "I will see you to your room, Ellis."

Alma made no protest but refused any assistance. He rose unsteadily and walked stiffly from the room, his friend at his side. When he reached his room he bade George good night, but George entered the room with him. Alma stood there bemused for a moment.

"Lie down, Ellis."

With profound relief after the hours of sitting, Alma did as he was bid. He showed a decided tendency to drift off to sleep, but George nudged him with a boot from the chair he was lounging in.

"My sister is very annoyed with you, Ellis," he offered by way of an introduction to their conversation.

"Well, I am very annoyed with her, too. Do you know what she did, George? She sent a message that I should dine with her in the dining parlor or not at all. Very inhospitable, George."

"Diana assures me that she resorted to such a measure only because of your disagreeable behavior," George said lazily.

"Wasn't disagreeable. Didn't feel like talking, was all."

"What has been going on here in my absence, Ellis?"

His friend regarded him with blurry eyes, and shook his head to clear it. "Haven't been making up to your sister, if that's what you think," he growled. "Treated her just as you do, you can be sure."

"Diana does not seem to think so. She accused you of black moods and assured me she has catered to your starts and stops for nearly a week."

"You have no idea how wretched it is not to be able

to sit down," his friend grumbled. "I apologized to her, several times, for my ill humor."

"Which merely means that you have shown it several times, I presume."

"Damnit, George, I could not ride a horse or drive a carriage! The day I sat that black of yours I reopened the wound. Fine animal, that. Want to sell him?"

"No, Ellis, I do not. My sister is a very tolerant woman, Ellis, but her concluding words to me were that she washes her hands of you."

"Well, I am glad of it," Alma replied bitterly. "She has taken me on walks to the village and the deer park, in addition to the stud farm. She has had me on the archery range. She has brought in infatuated suitors to entertain me at fencing and billiards. She has had me singing with her in the music room. She has taken me fishing. She has had a chariot built for me. She has dragged me to an insipid country affair with a dragon countess. It is high time she left me alone!"

"I see. I must compliment her on her perseverance. I have never known you to be churlish, Ellis. Surely you can see that she only wished to keep you from being bored and dwelling on your injury."

"Of course I can see that!" Alma roared. "I should be grateful to her! I *am* grateful to her! Now I want her to leave me alone!" Alma's face set in grim lines, and George sighed.

"Very well, Ellis. We will talk more in the morning. I will send your man to you. Good night."

"George . . ."

"Yes?"

"I . . . no, let us talk tomorrow. My head hurts."

"I'm not surprised," George said unfeelingly.

"A moment later he tapped on his sister's door and called softly to her. She invited him in and hastily wiped away the last of the tears she had shed.

"I hope you have not been crying because you thought I scolded you," he remarked as he took a seat beside her bed.

"I know you will always look at both sides before

94

you place blame, George. I know I am not entirely faultless, but I was grievously provoked."

"I can understand that now. I have heard from Ellis's own lips how you have endeavored to entertain him." He stared at the wardrobe for a moment before continuing. "He is grateful to you, Diana, but seems to be suffering from a very real irritation of the nerves."

"I worked so hard to get him out of the sullens, George. I have had no time to myself at all, what with Alma and Mrs. Lewis. She did not deserve to be left entirely to her own devices, even though she is perfectly happy to embroider all day. Yesterday Alma was finally at peace with me it seemed, since he could drive the chariot. Then last night and today he was all stuffy again."

"You have both mentioned a chariot. You had one made? A Roman-style chariot?" George asked, a smile spreading across his face.

"Yes," Diana responded with a grin. "It is marvellous, George. The young men were racing it all day today. It almost always wins because it's so light."

"I look forward to seeing it. That was very clever of you, my dear. I knew it would blue-devil Ellis to be kept away from horses. It seems he didn't either, because he mentioned riding the black."

"Oh, that was awful. He had calmed the horse considerably and could not pass up the right moment to mount him, George, but his face absolutely drained of blood when he sat him. I had to bite my lip, but I did not say a word, either."

"Well, you have nothing with which to reproach yourself, love. Even dinner, given the circumstances. I will keep him out of your way until he leaves, but I want you to understand that he is not ordinarily like this. Usually he is very easygoing, personable and polite."

"If you say so, George," she answered skeptically. "There were times when he was very nice indeed, I must admit." She sighed, and then her face took on an anxious look. "Will you tell me about Miss Sanfield now?"

"There is not much to tell, Diana. When I arrived in

town I read of her engagement and went the next day to call on her, but she had left town. I foolishly assumed that she had gone to her home near Lymington and took myself off there, losing a day because of rain. There is something strange about the engagement, but I cannot put my finger on it. Alonna has gone to her sister near Colchester."

"And you did not go there?" she asked, puzzled.

"Really, my dear, I have gone too far already. What good will it do if she is engaged? And if she is not, the announcement should be retracted. I do not want to harass the poor girl."

"But, George, you told me she doesn't know of your intentions. If she is in difficulties, you should be the one to see she comes right."

"You forget that I do not know if she would welcome my assistance."

"You can only find out if you ask her," his sister pointed out.

"I think I will await events, Diana. When and if a retraction is published I will approach her. I do not think I should do more now."

"But . . ."

"No, my dear. Let us leave it at that. She will be safe with her sister."

"Do I know her sister?"

"I should think not. She is Lady Trafford. Cranmer said she is just delivered of twins."

"How nice." Diana studied her brother's face for a moment. "It must be very difficult for you to wait, George."

"Nonsense," he replied bracingly, as he rose from his chair and placed a salute on her cheek. "Thank you for the care you have taken of Ellis, Diana. I am truly sorry he has been such a wretch."

"I was happy to do it for you, George."

Diana did not ordinarily interfere in her brother's life, just as he did not interfere in hers. When he had left her for the night, though, she considered what he had told her and decided that perhaps she would do just a little something this time. Colchester could not be more than five and twenty miles distant, as the crow flew. She left word with her maid that she wished to be called at seven the next morning.

chapter eleven

For a moment Diana did not remember why she had asked to be awakened at such an hour. She raised sleepy eyes questioningly at her maid and then she recalled the previous night's discussion. "Annie, I wish you to inform the stable that I want my phaeton ready in half an hour. Have some chocolate and toast sent up for me, please. I will dress myself."

When the maid left, Diana chose an attractive dress which fit her properly, and managed to arrange her hair in a less severe style than was her custom. It was a habit with George to bring her some fashionable frippery each time he returned, and the very fact that he had not done so on this occasion indicated to her the depth of his distraction. Not that she minded not receiving a present; far from it. It was his way of prodding her to modishness and part of the game they unspeakably played about her determination not to draw attention to her beauty. For she was forced then to wear each of the items he brought at the appropriate time, and it was a nuisance for her. Not that she blamed him. Who would want a dowd for a sister? But she thought she knew herself well enough that her small deception was useful, if no longer necessary. And it was effective, yesterday was a good example. She had dressed to the nines for the Dodges' entertainment, and look at all the young men who had come to call the day after! But they would not long pester her after she appeared looking very ordinary at their races. She sometimes wondered what her neighbors thought of her, but she seldom worried about it.

Nonetheless, if she was going to meet George's young woman, Diana had no intention of shaming him. She chose a coat with a triple collar and wide cuffs with lace ruffles, and a high crowned hat with a small brim, both in emerald green. She ate the toast and drank the chocolate which had arrived by this time, and then presented herself at the stables.

Jenkins had her phaeton ready but looked intent on discovering her destination. She climbed up onto the seat with his help, Josh jumped on behind, and she airily told Jenkins that she would be gone for the better part of the day to visit friends, and please to advise her brother of the fact. Before he could make any demur she flicked her whip and drove off. She knew the road to Haverhill well and kept her matched grays at an easy pace as she did not wish to make any change of team unless it was strictly necessary. The weather was fine and she could see bright spring flowers in bloom about the cottages and farms she passed. Once through Haverhill she followed the road to Halstead, where she paused to rest the horses and refresh herself and Josh at the inn. She enquired of the landlord if he knew where Lady Trafford lived and he proved all helpfulness. Yes, he knew Trafford Hall and he could direct her there if she needed his assistance. She was more than happy to accept his offer and set off confident of her destination. The maze of lanes he had directed her through, however, soon had her confused, and Josh had not overheard the landlord's, directions, but she eventually asked directions of a field hand and found that she had not far to go.

When she arrived at the Hall, a groom came running to assist Josh with her carriage and she proceeded to the door which the groom indicated in the side of one of its two main projections. She handed a card to the butler and asked if she might see Miss Alonna Sanfield. The hour was still early, and for a while she had considered delaying her arrival, but her curiosity and the desire to return to the Park at a reasonable hour had prompted her to proceed. "If the family is still at breakfast, please do not disturb them," she urged the butler. She was shown into the Red Parlor and seated herself comfortably on an upholstered settee in expectation of a considerable wait.

Within minutes, however, a blond young lady appeared at the door and smiled shyly at her. "Miss Savile?" she asked quietly.

"Yes, I am Diana, George Savile's sister. I had hoped I might have a word with you."

Alonna came into the room and shook hands with her visitor. "I have wanted to meet you. Mr. Savile speaks highly of you, but he says you rarely come to town."

"George is prejudiced in my favor," Diana replied, "and he is very indulgent. You must not put too much reliance on what he says about me."

"I should think not!" Alonna replied indignantly. "He never even mentioned how lovely you were."

"I should not think he notices my looks much. Miss Sanfield, I noticed in the paper the other day that you are engaged to Lord Vallert."

Alonna sighed. "Lord Vallert put the notice in the paper without my consent, Miss Savile. I have informed him that he is to have it removed."

"Then you are not to marry him? You do not wish to marry him?"

"No, nor ever have. It was very wrong of him and he did it in a fit of pique. My father should have removed it immediately, but he did not. If Lord Vallert does not do so within the next few days, I shall have to handle the matter myself," she said sadly.

"How very cruel of him to put you through such a thing!"

"He had always seemed nice enough until I refused his offer." Alonna chucked in remembrance of the scene. "He could not believe that I would turn him down."

"I have a suitor like that," Diana laughed, "full of so much self-consequence that he continues to believe that I have heard him wrong or simply cannot believe my good fortune." The two women shared an amused glance.

"Is your brother well, Miss Savile?"

"Yes, he arrived at the Park last evening. He . . ." Diana stopped abruptly. It would not be fair to George to say anything further to the young woman at this point. "I understand your sister has recently been safely delivered of twins."

Alonna's eyes shone with excitement. "Oh, Miss

Savile, I was there during the confinement and it was the most miraculous event. I must show you the babies, and introduce you to my sister." She rose and extended her hand to Diana, who took it and tucked it through her arm as they climbed the grand staircase. "I have a nephew Mark, as well, who is two. Later I will take you to the nursery to meet him." She tapped on her sister's door and was invited to enter.

"Margaret, I have someone with me," she said, as she peeped around the door.

"Come in, Alonna. I should like to meet your friend," Margaret assured her as she noticed Diana behind her sister. It crossed her mind that the young woman was somehow familiar.

"This is Diana Savile, Margaret, Mr. George Savile's sister."

"I have met your brother in London, Miss Savile, and am pleased to meet you. There is some resemblance between you."

"I thought so, too," Alonna admitted, "when I came into the Red Parlor."

Margaret turned to her sister in confusion. "You have only just met Miss Savile?"

"Yes, Margaret, she has come . . ." Alonna herself was not quite sure why Diana had come and her voice died.

"I have come to invite Miss Sanfield to spend a few days with me at the Park," Diana suggested, surprising herself.

"You have?" Alonna asked incredulously.

Margaret regarded the two of them indulgently. "Why, I think that's a perfectly lovely idea. We've been working Alonna far too hard these last few days, and to tell the truth, my mother-in-law wishes to take over her activities. She feels left out since she missed the actual birth," Margaret explained.

Alonna was still staring at Diana in amazement, but Diana smiled and said, "Yes, for George has the most obstreperous guest and I wish to stay out of his way until he leaves. Perhaps you know him, Miss Sanfield? Lord Alma?"

"Lord Alma? Obstreperous? Why, I have never known him to be anything but truly gallant and cheerful."

"So George tells me, too, but it has been otherwise during his stay. You see, I accidentally shot him with an arrow, and then George had to go off to London to . . . well, he had to leave, and so I was left to entertain Lord Alma. Only he has been unable to sit and it seems to irritate him unreasonably. So when George mentioned that you were so close by, and he had told me about you, I thought that I should like to meet you. You would be doing me a great favor to come, you know," Diana said beseechingly. "Perhaps Lord Alma would even improve if you were there."

"You shot him with an arrow?" Margaret broke into delighted laughter. "How marvellous!"

"I am beginning to think so, too, Lady Trafford," Diana retorted with acerbity.

Margaret turned to her sister and said gently, "I think you should go, love."

"But . . . when should I come?" Alonna asked.

"I would like to take you with me when I leave," Diana urged her.

"The two sisters shared a glance and Margaret nodded. "Go and pack a portmanteau, my dear. Miss Savile and I will enjoy a chat."

Bemused, Alonna left the room. Margaret turned to Diana and smiled. "Why did you really come, Miss Savile?"

"Well, George has been dashing all over the countryside to learn what he could of Miss Sanfield's engagement. A friend of his in London thought it very strange, since your father would not acknowledge it, and I came to learn the truth of it."

"Why did your brother not come?"

"He thought at first Miss Sanfield had gone to Lymington and he went there. I believe he feels rather foolish for being so impulsive; he is not usually. And then he did not wish to approach her if she was engaged. He told me that he would wait to see what happened."

"So he does not know you are here?"

"No, and I should not be. George has always allowed me to run my own life and I owe him the same courtesy, but he has determined on a course of being *gentlemanly* and heaven knows where that will lead. I have no intention of saying a word of this to Miss Sanfield, of course. She will be my guest, and I shall take good care of her. I have Mrs. Lewis from the village staying with me, too, because Lord Alma could not stay there without her. I cannot think she will have gone back to her home yet."

Margaret accepted this flow of information calmly and said, "I like your brother, Miss Savile." She would have said more, but a tap at the door brought in the nursery maid with a baby in each arm. Diana rose to look at the infants and congratulate their mother. A small boy burst through the door and stopped abruptly when he saw the visitor. Margaret called him over to her and hugged him before saying, "Mark, this is Miss Savile, a friend of your Aunt Alonna's. Your aunt is going to stay with her for a few days."

Mark gravely shook hands with Diana and asked where she lived. "Not so very far away, about five miles from Haverhill, Mark."

Lord Trafford entered then to retrieve his son and was introduced to Diana. He also knew her brother and sent his regards. His surprise on hearing that Alonna was leaving to spend some time at the Park was quickly hidden when his wife threw him a warning glance. He did not stay long, but swung his son on his shoulder and said they must not keep the horses waiting.

When Alonna returned, she quietly announced that her portmanteau was packed. She clung to her sister for a moment, and Margaret smiled encouragingly before the two young women ordered the phaeton brought round and set out for the Park.

George took an early ride before entering the breakfast parlor where he found Mrs. Lewis and Alma already partaking of their meal. "I have seen your chariot, Ellis, and hear that it beats a phaeton every time."

"Yes, your sister suggested that it might be a more

103

even race if the chariot were pulled by a single horse."
Alma glanced at Diana's empty seat and raised a brow in
query to his host.

"Jenkins tells me that Diana has left for the day to
visit friends. She has been rather housebound of late and
could stand the diversion, I dare say."

Alma flushed and Mrs. Lewis said timidly, "Do you
think I should go home now, Mr. Savile?"

"No, I hope you will stay on a while. I cannot be
sure if I will have to leave again, and Diana will be
grateful for your company. I am glad you could come on
such short notice."

"It has been a pleasure, sir," Mrs. Lewis assured
him. "I was included in the invitation to the Dodges'
party and it was a rare treat for me." She proceeded to
tell him of how elegant his sister had looked and what the
entertainment had consisted of, and when she had finished her meal (and her monologue) she left the two men
in the breakfast parlor to make her way to her embroidery.

Alma and George had been friends for some ten
years, but when they were left alone silence reigned in the
room. In general, George was very tolerant of the behavior of his friends, but he was surprised and exasperated
by the accounts he had heard of the relations between his
sister and his guest. Alma was at a loss to explain his
irascibility; he did not understand it himself. The injury
had seemed a gruesome joke at first, but he had been
completely thrown out of stride when Diana had been
exposed to his nakedness while she removed the arrow.
Heaven knew he had been naked with enough women,
but never in such a situation and never with an imperious
young woman of quality. And then the enforced standing
had proved more burdensome than he could have imagined at the start. If she had not been so patient with him
it might not have been so difficult, but in the face of all
his petty bitterness she had provided him with the chariot,
which indicated that she understood how he chafed at
being unable to ride and drive.

They *had* reached some accord then, but it was
shattered by her appearance for the Dodges' party. Again

he had felt put-upon, deceived, a fool. For a week he had been consorting with the "younger brother" George had offered him, and suddenly he found that she was a goddess in disguise. A goddess who had taken an arrow from his bottom. He could not forgive her that.

George and Alma sat in the breakfast parlor for some time after they had finished eating. Finally Alma spoke almost diffidently. "I will leave today if you want me to, George. There is no excuse I can give you for my behavior. I wish to God I had never come!"

"No, I don't want you to leave until you will be comfortable sitting in a carriage. I can see that you are in some pain right now. Come, we'll talk while we walk to the stables."

Alma felt better once he was on his feet and he remembered why George had left the Park in the first place. "I was sorry to read of Miss Sanfield's engagement, George."

"There is some mystery about it, Ellis. Her father does not acknowledge it."

"Really? Perhaps Vallert is toying with the settlement."

"I have no idea." In his present mood George had no intention of telling Alma any more about the situation. There was little more to tell in any case.

"Did you try the chariot?"

"No, but I should like to."

The two men spent the morning around the stables and the afternoon at the stud farm. They only returned to the house in time for tea late in the afternoon, and found Diana, changed back to her usual attire, seated with Mrs. Lewis in the small parlor.

George greeted her fondly, asking, "Did you have a good day away from home, love?"

"Perfect, George. But I must speak with you alone for a moment for I have brought a visitor."

With slightly raised brows, he gave in to the urgency her eyes spoke. "If you will excuse us a moment, Mrs. Lewis, Ellis."

Diana nodded gravely to Alma as she followed her brother from the room. In the library George waved her to a seat. "Who is your guest, and where is she, or he, as the case may be?"

"She is in her room, George, and she is Alonna Sanfield." Diana hurried on at her brother's profoundly shocked expression. "I did not originally intend to bring her back with me, you understand, just to find out what I could about the engagement. Vallert inserted the announcement against her express wishes, and he and her father have both refused to renounce it. She intends to do so herself if Vallert does not take care of the matter soon. She never agreed to marry him, and she does not wish to marry him." Diana fell quiet when her brother raised a silencing hand.

"You must be learning bad habits from Ellis, Diana. I am surprised that you would involve yourself in my affairs," he said sternly.

Diana bit her lip to keep from crying. It was very seldom that her brother censured her. "I know, George," she whispered. "I promise you I told her nothing except that you had mentioned her to me and that she was close by. I used Alma as an excuse for inviting her here. I did tell her sister a bit more," she admitted sadly, "for I wanted her to understand the situation. Lord Trafford sent you his regards. Alonna is aware that you did not know I was going to her."

For some time after his sister finished speaking, George studied his hands. "Very well, Diana," he said without looking up. "Bring her down to tea."

Diana escaped from the room as quickly as she could, but in the hall she paused to compose herself. It was many years since she had incurred George's displeasure to such a degree and she felt thoroughly shaken. Whatever had possessed her to carry out such a scheme! She might have known, she in fact *had* known, that George would not like it. If George had been willing to see the outcome in his own time, she should have accepted his decision. Her heart heavy, she climbed the stairs to her new friend's room.

When they entered the small parlor Diana saw Alma's eyes widen with astonishment. George took Alonna's hand and smiled gravely. "I am so glad Diana has brought you to the Park, Alonna. I believe you know Lord Alma, and this is Mrs. Lewis, our neighbor in Linton."

Alonna acknowledged the introduction and accepted a cup of tea from Mrs. Lewis. George seated himself beside her on the sofa and asked, "Is your sister well? I understand she is recently delivered of twins."

"Oh, Margaret is thriving, and they are the most adorable babies. My nephew is the tiniest bit jealous, I fear, but my brother-in-law is keeping him busy."

"And your father is well?" George persisted.

"Yes, when last I saw him."

"I understand the announcement of your engagement was erroneous and that it is to be retracted," George said gently, but implacably. Diana could have kicked him for bringing up the subject at all.

But Alonna seemed quite capable of handling the situation. Without a blink she replied, "Yes, very unfortunate. I fear Lord Vallert allowed his imagination to run away with him." She smiled sweetly at George as though mocking him for his exercise.

George grinned then and would have bestowed a kiss on her if there had not been others present. "Well done," he murmured appreciatively.

Diana, who had spent the morning and the afternoon's drive with a young woman who appeared all amiability but slightly shy, was surprised and pleased at the poise with which she accepted George's interrogation, one which she would no doubt undergo dozens of times when she returned to London. It also relieved Diana's mind somewhat of the burden of George's censure; he was pleased with Miss Sanfield and therefore more likely to forgive his sister her blunder.

With a wicked grin indicating that it served them both right, George offered to show Alonna around the house and grounds, and he left his sister and his friend to fend for themselves. Mrs. Lewis had begun to nod in her chair and Diana wished to allow her a catnap in peace, so she gestured to Alma to follow her, and left the room.

They stood awkwardly together in the hall and eventually he stiffly asked her if she would care for a game of billiards, and Diana acquiesced.

While they were playing Alma commented blandly, "I was not aware that you knew Miss Sanfield."

After Diana completed an accurate cushion shot, she returned just as blandly, "I met her only today."

"How fortuitous," he remarked, his voice laden with sarcasm.

"It is no concern of yours, Lord Alma." Diana chalked her cue and did not meet his gaze.

"I imagine George did not like it," he prodded.

"No, it was foolish of me," she admitted readily, as she missed her shot and stood up. "He said I was picking up bad habits from you."

Alma's eyes flashed for a moment, and then the humor of the situation was borne in on him and he laughed. "So we are both in his black books, are we? Well, he is pleased to have Miss Sanfield here all the same, so you need not worry. Were you curious as to the outcome, Diana?" There was no sarcasm this time, merely amusement.

With a hesitant smile she accepted his peace offering. "I suppose that was it in part, but I was also concerned for her. It seemed she might be in trouble, to have left town so abruptly and with her father refusing to acknowledge the engagement."

They had stopped playing their game now and stood facing each other. "How did the announcement get printed?" he asked.

"Alonna had refused Vallert and he placed it in spite of her. Her father would not refute it, hoping that she would feel it necessary to marry Vallert. A very uncomfortable situation, I fear. She has given Vallert a week to have it repudiated; if he does not, she will do so herself."

"So it would all have been taken care of without you," he remarked gently.

"Yes, of course," she replied over a lump in her throat. "But you know, Alma, I could not be sure that her sister would support her. I was not acquainted with

Lady Trafford, and women who have just borne children are not always . . . perfectly rational."

"You have known a lot of women after they have borne children?" he asked skeptically.

"You forget that I assist Mr. Thatcher," she retorted. "Sometimes women are very low for several months, or so wrapped up in the new baby that they do not pay much attention to anything else. Lady Trafford was not like that—she was very chipper and interested in her sister's problems."

Alma leaned over the table to make a shot. "A nice woman. I always liked her."

"Yes, she and Alonna both seemed surprised by my description of you."

He looked up startled. "Whatever did you say to them, wretched girl?"

"Well, I had to have some reason to invite Alonna home with me, so I told her I needed company to keep me away from George's obstreperous guest."

Alma cast his eyes heavenward. "You are intent on destroying me, are you not, Diana? Not satisfied with wounding my body, you are determined to ruin my reputation as well."

"I am sure," she retorted pertly, "that if you behave yourself while Alonna is here your reputation will be saved."

"Thank God," he murmured soulfully. "Your shot."

chapter twelve

When George and Alonna had completed the tour of the house, they traversed the balustraded terraces. There was no lack of dialogue between them; they were as at ease together as they had been on each of their previous encounters. It was a wonder to both of them, but when they were together they accepted it. Alonna had been as pleased as Diana that she had been able to cope with George's interrogation over tea, but she had found on former occasions that merely being with him gave her courage. Now she spoke cheerfully of being at the birth of the twins, not in the least worried that he would be shocked.

"Diana has spoken of the confinements she has attended with a sort of wonder," George mused. "I imagine it must seem rather miraculous."

"It does. I felt so proud for Margaret, and when Phillip came in he was all concern for her and did not even glance at the babies until she urged him to."

"A very proper sentiment," George replied with a grin. "I am sure I shall feel the same when I marry and my wife produces a child."

For the first time in his company Alonna felt slightly nervous and turned her head to study the yew hedges. George gazed down on her tenderly and reached out a hand to touch her arm and draw her attention to him. She offered him a tremulous smile but met his eyes unwaveringly.

"Alonna, I should, of course, approach your father first, but I have been running about the countryside to no purpose for several days, and your father is not making himself available. Will you do me the honor of becoming my wife?"

"Yes, George," she said softly.

"Then I will forgive Diana for her interference," he laughed as he drew Alonna into his arms and kissed her.

"I have wanted to do that for a very long time," he confessed.

"And I have wanted you to," she replied shyly. "Is it acceptable for me to tell you so?"

"You are to tell me exactly what you wish to at any time, my love. I *have* told you that I love you, have I not?"

"No, George, I do not believe that you have."

He kissed her again, this time until she was breathless. "Well, I do, you know. I was come to town to offer for you when I read of your engagement. When I learned that you had left town I assumed that you had gone to Lymington and I went there." He wryly acknowledged her surprised expression. "I do not know exactly what I intended to say to you. Your butler there told me that you might have gone to Colchester, so I went back to London, where a friend of mine said your father had refused to acknowledge your engagement when he spoke of it."

"That is something to Papa's credit, I suppose," she remarked dryly.

"Yes, he does not show in the best light in this muddle. Will he have any objection to me as your husband?"

"I should think not. He only wishes to marry me off as soon as possible," she replied sadly.

"Poor love."

"I do not mind so much now, George. Why did you not come to Colchester?"

"I thought better of it. If the engagement was a hoax, I thought it wiser to wait until a retraction was printed before approaching you. And if it was real, well, then there was no possibility of approaching you at all."

"I see. So you were angry with Diana for bringing me here?" She raised doubtful eyes to his.

"Alonna, you must understand that I did not wish to cause you any distress. In the first agony of reading of your engagement I felt I must speak with you to be sure it was something you wanted, that you were not being forced into it. When I knew you were with your sister, whom I have met and hold in high esteem, and that your father did not acknowledge the engagement, I thought it would be more proper for me to await events."

"It was not that you had thought better of marrying me? I know I am very young and inexperienced compared with you, George. I should not like to think that Diana forced your hand." She dropped her eyes to her hands which were plucking nervously at her gown.

George lifted her chin gently with his finger. "Alonna, that is precisely *why* I was angry with Diana. Because you might think she had forced me into a position I did not wish to be in." George hugged her to him for a moment and then set her aside to say, "I have not been able to be in town to see you as much as I wanted. It was necessary for me to join a friend on a trip to Paris and then later to attend his wedding. But what with one thing and another, I had not had the opportunity to assure you of my intentions. I did not like your not knowing," he said simply.

Alonna's eyes sparkled with tears. "It was awful not knowing, George."

"Forgive me, my love. It will not happen again. I could not be sure that you would have me, that I was the right man for you."

"I love you, George."

"Now that is something I find highly acceptable for you to tell me," he said with a grin. "Come, love, it is time we changed for dinner. I should not leave Diana and Alma in each other's company too long."

"Why not?" she asked as they began to walk back toward the house.

"There is a great deal of friction between them. Last night Diana sent him a message that he would eat his meal in the dining parlor or not at all," he informed her seriously, but his eyes danced.

"How delightful! I cannot think he would like such an ultimatum."

"No more did he. But they will have to rub along together for a few more days because I have no intention of sharing you with either of them now that I have you here."

George found, however, when the whole house party

was gathered for dinner, that his sister and friend had apparently declared a truce. He shrugged helplessly at Alonna when she cast him a look of query. Throughout the evening Diana and Alma continued on the easiest of terms, and exhibited every intent of allowing George as much time with Alonna as he could wish.

Delighted by the successful conclusion to her day's activities, Diana felicitated Alonna on her engagement. When George was alone with his sister before she went to bed he said, "I did not mean to be so hard on you earlier, Diana, but this was very important to me and I did not wish to see anything go awry."

"It was my fault, George, and I should not have done it. But I'm glad I did," she added with an impish grin.

"So am I." He saluted her cheek and hugged her to him. "I know you were concerned for me, love, but I beg you will not do such a thing again."

"I won't," she promised. "Good night, George. I am very happy for you."

As the memory of Diana's appearance in evening dress dimmed for Alma, he was able to accept her again on the footing they had gained before that disastrous evening. George and Alonna were able to spend the next several days getting to know each other better as Diana and Alma took up the pastimes they had pursued during George's absence. Chariot racing, archery and walks about the estate kept them harmlessly occupied while George and Alonna rode and talked. Mrs. Lewis moved out into the garden on the warmer days to work her needle in the sun, happily surveying the young people about their activities. Alma now attempted short drives in the phaeton and found that he was mending rapidly.

One morning when Alma and Diana were driving together a child darted out into the lane and waved them to a halt. The boy, his face stained with tears and dirt, turned to Diana and begged, "Oh, please, Miss Savile, my Daddy is hurt bad and we cannot find Mr. Thatcher. Would you come to him?"

"Of course, Peter." She reached down her hand to

him and drew him up onto her lap, at the same time directing Alma to a farm off to the left down a narrow, rutted lane. The boy clung to her and she patted his shoulders gently while she assured him that she would do what she could, and Alma regarded them with concern. When they arrived at the neat stone farmhouse with its tidy rows of spring flowers, he leaped out and handed down first the child and then Diana.

"Should I come with you?" he asked.

"Yes, if you will. You may be of assistance."

Peter led them into the house, calling for his mother in an anxious voice. A harassed woman in her thirties hurried out into the hall. Her dress was covered with blood and she was white-faced but when she saw Diana the anxiety in her eyes was replaced by a measure of relief. "Oh, thank God, he has found you, Miss Savile. Will you come to Mr. Green? He was ploughing when the accident occurred. There is a sharp stone still sticking in him and I cannot remove it."

Diana nodded and followed Mrs. Green into the bedroom where her husband lay on the bed writhing in agony. Diana pulled back the blanket to examine the wound, which was on his side just below the waist. The stone indeed was still lodged there, but blood continued to ooze out around it. The man was naked.

Fascinated, Alma watched as Diana flung her bonnet on a chair and drew up another to seat herself at the man's side and feel about the stone with careful fingers. Then she began to give calm, low-voiced instructions to Mrs. Green to bring more cloths and hot water, in addition to a clean knife and some astringent. When these had been assembled she instructed Alma to hold the man's hands firmly while she worked to dislodge the stone with the knife. The stone was several inches long and deeply embedded in the man's flesh. Perspiration broke out on her forehead as she gently, carefully worked the stone toward her; Mrs. Green dried her brow anxiously during the process, and Mr. Green fainted after a few minutes. Alma felt relieved that the man did not feel more of the pain caused by the removal.

When Diana had the stone out she looked around at

Mrs. Green and said, "I cannot be sure if it pierced anything important, Mrs. Green. I don't think so, but you will have to have Mr. Thatcher look at it. In the meantime I will bind it so that the bleeding will stop." She continued to work efficiently as she spoke, drops of blood falling on the gray muslin dress she wore. They did not seem to concern her, and eventually she stood up and washed her hands in a basin set nearby. "That is all I can do myself. Your husband will be in pain and Mr. Thatcher may wish to prescribe something for him. Peter said you could not find the apothecary."

"No, ma'am. My eldest is still out trying, but it seems there was a difficult confinement and an accident as well, and he might be at either."

"When he comes, tell him what I have done and he should send for me if he has any questions." Diana reached down to pick up her bonnet and tuck her hair under it.

"Do you . . . think Mr. Green will be all right?" the woman asked in a frightened voice.

"Yes, I think so. You must watch for fever, though, and change the binding carefully and keep the wound clean." Diana squeezed the woman's hand encouragingly and headed for the bedroom door.

Alma followed Diana, who gently accepted the woman's thanks. When they were in the phaeton again he immediately set the horses in motion, but drew them in again when they were a short way down the lane, for Diana had put her head down in her lap and was taking great mouthfuls of air.

"Are you all right, Diana?" he asked anxiously.

She did not answer him for a few minutes, but he could see that her bonnet moved as she nodded slightly. Eventually she raised her head and he could see that her face was pale. Her words were a whisper when she admitted, "I do what I can, Alma, and Mr. Thatcher is generally pleased with me, but I have a tendency to faint or be sick afterwards."

He stared at her mortified face with amazement. "You were as calm as could be while you worked on him. I thought *I* would be sick."

Diana smiled shakily. "Mr. Thatcher says so long as I do not faint while there is still something to be done, it is enough, but you would think I would become used to it, and I never do."

"Well, for God's sake, Diana, all that blood was enough to turn the stomach of a horse!"

"I should be used to it," she reiterated emphatically.

"Did you faint after you operated on me?" he asked curiously.

"No, I was sick," she replied softly.

Alma gave a burst of laughter. "I think, then, that I may consider forgiving you. Does George know that you do not feel well after your surgical feats?"

"No, and you are not to tell him, Alma," she pleaded. "He might not allow me to help Mr. Thatcher any longer, and sometimes I am truly needed, as I was today."

"Very well, I will not speak of it." He urged the horses forward again as she smiled with relief. "Did you tell Mrs. Green the truth when you said you thought nothing important had been damaged?"

"Yes, but I don't know enough to be sure. Mr. Thatcher will be able to tell her more, I hope."

They rode in silence for some time, Alma shifting uncomfortably on his seat. "It is awful when someone dies," she whispered.

He looked at her searchingly. "You have seen people die?"

"Yes. A child once, and an old woman. The woman I did not mind so much for she looked forward to her death as a release from pain, but the child . . ."

"Perhaps you should not work with Mr. Thatcher, Diana."

She sighed. "I don't, so very often. I could not refuse to help when I was needed, could I?"

"I suppose not," Alma replied gruffly, as he thought that although he could think of many people who would, Diana he could not picture doing so.

After a moment Diana brightened. "But there are the confinements, too. There is something very special about them, you know. Everyone is so pleased and excited when a baby is born. Alonna saw her sister's twins delivered."

Alma shook his head in mock bewilderment. "Whatever happened to the shy young maidens I used to meet who knew nothing of all these matters?"

"You will find them when you return to London, no doubt," she suggested helpfully, her eyes twinkling.

"I dare say," he retorted grudgingly. "Back to the normal world." For just a moment the idea was disappointing, but he shrugged off the thought. He had plans for his stay in the metropolis.

Since Diana's morning had been somewhat upsetting for her Alma suggested that they go fishing after luncheon. The spring sun was warm and Alma fell asleep, his head cradled on his crossed arms. Diana removed the pole from his hand and set it beside him. She watched the water ripple over rocks and around outcroppings of the bank, and occasionally felt a tug on her rod, but there was not much activity. Rogue had followed them to the river and lay curled up against Alma. Diana smiled at the picture they made, Alma with his dark hair curling on his forehead and the dog thumping a bushy tail in his sleep.

When Alma awoke he lazily shifted over onto his back, carefully, and watched the clouds scudding past the trees far overhead. His gaze then fell on Diana and he asked, "Did you think of a new project?"

"No."

"Were you thinking this morning?"

"No."

"Making plans for George's wedding?"

"No."

"Surely you have not sat there just . . . feeling good?" he asked mockingly, his eyes dancing.

"You need not scoff, Alma," she returned. "I do not fall asleep at the blink of an eye the way you do."

"Too bad," he replied as he stretched his legs leisurely. "It is a knack."

"You share your talent with Rogue," she pointed out.

Alma watched the dog gravely. "But I don't wag my tail when I sleep."

"How do you know?" she asked impishly.

He regarded her sternly. "Even if I did, which I doubt, it would not be proper for you to mention it."

"Well, I am glad you told me. I should not wish to say anything improper to you."

"Of course not," he agreed, but he could contain his laughter no longer, and his merriment woke the dog, who began barking.

Diana shook her head with exasperation at the two of them. "You cannot expect me to take my lessons in decorum seriously, Alma, if you carry on like that. Hush, Rogue."

The dog trotted over to her where she sat with her arms clasped about her knees, her skirts swirling around her. Rogue waved the plume of his tail gaily and she hugged him briefly before allowing Alma to pull her to her feet. The scarcity of their catch did not daunt them, and they returned to the house in perfect charity.

When George mentioned to Alma later that afternoon that they would be celebrating Diana's birthday at dinner, Alma felt annoyed that he had not learned earlier of the event and slipped off to the village to see what he could find. The items he considered—parasols, hair combs, purses and fans as well as shawls and gloves—merely reminded him that such items would probably be used when she was dressed as she had for the Dodges' party, and he dismissed them. He remembered that she had a love of old books, and if he had been at Stillings he might have found her something of special interest, but here in Linton there was little hope of securing an interesting volume. Diana herself had said that she went to Cambridge for such items. Nevertheless, he began to make queries in the shops and eventually unearthed a volume on medicinal herbs which the proprietor of the linen drapers found artfully resting with several other volumes in a window draped with sample materials. Alma considered its age and condition so carefully that the proprietor quickly doubled the price he had originally considered charging, but Alma cheerfully paid him what the volume was worth, a gesture which made the man's eyes widen. When Alma had strolled out of the shop, the proprietor eagerly surveyed the remaining volumes, only to find them totally uninteresting editions of not-so-current gothic novels.

George had urged his sister to dress for dinner in a style befitting the occasion, and she reluctantly agreed. Alma received the transformation stoically, and Alonna realized for the first time that since the day she had met Diana her friend had dressed rather plainly. The small golden circlet and arrow set with stones which Alonna had chosen for her future sister-in-law was laughingly accepted as the perfect gift for an archer. George presented Diana with a beautifully tooled, leather jewelry case and then rose to propose a toast to her.

"No, wait," Alma protested. "I have a present for her, too." He reached under his chair where he had hidden the small volume and handed it to her with an embarrassed smile. "Happy birthday, Diana."

She took the book carefully from him and her eyes opened in surprise. "Why, it's beautiful, Alma. How kind of you!"

"It seemed appropriate." He smiled as she fingered the volume with loving hands.

Puzzled as to how his friend had come up with such a present on so short notice, George was nonetheless pleased that he had made the effort. Diana's real delight in the gift was evident, and Alma seemed willing to accept her this time in her modish silver and lace gown, so George proceeded, with an easy mind, with the toast he had intended.

chapter thirteen

The next morning Alma surprised Diana by saying, "I think I shall be ready to leave tomorrow. It will take the better part of the day to reach London with all the stops I will have to make, but I think I can manage it now."

"Truly? There is no need for you to leave if you are not yet ready."

"I am eager to get to London. I've been here almost two weeks now."

"I hope you will see Allison and Walter in town. I shall miss them for the next few months."

"No one to play with, Diana?" he teased her.

"Too true," she retorted. "George does not let anyone else have a moment with Alonna, and now you are leaving, too," she said sadly.

"There are the books on the Middle Ages to read."

"Yes," she agreed. "You will not mind if I keep them a while?"

"Keep them as long as you wish. They merely gather dust at Stillings."

They were companionably silent for a while and then Alma remembered something. "You have never reminded me that I promised to fence with you if you taught me archery. Shall we have a bout this morning?"

Diana's face lit. "You would not mind? I am not very good at it, Alma, and will not provide you with much sport."

"I promised, as I recall," he grumbled good-naturedly. "Half an hour, in the Long Gallery?"

Having given up hope of fencing with Alma, Diana in her enthusiasm did not pause to consider the wisdom of wearing her fencing outfit. She always wore it with George, and he was the only one she fenced with. It did not occur to her that in itself it was very flattering to her, if perhaps improper. She arrived at the Long Gallery in a frilled shirt and blue knitted breeches which extended to just below her knees. Her stockings, as the rest of her outfit, were items which George had discarded as a youth and she had found in the attics. The white stockings had clocks and she wore them with her own blue slippers, which she removed for her lessons. In preparation for wearing a mask she had tumbled her hair on top of her head and pinned it there securely.

Alma was in the Long Gallery before her and watched her approach down the room. A flush came to his cheeks as he remembered George's remarks about his sister's fencing outfit. The frilled shirt was a trifle small over her breasts but fit snugly otherwise. The knee breeches and stockings were molded to her elegant legs and behind. Really, it was hardly decent for her to appear before him in such an outfit. Without a word, but managing a hasty smile, he handed her a mask and a padded jacket to don. She cheerfully did so, unaware of his turmoil, and picked up a buttoned foil.

After the salute he sternly schooled himself to concentrate on teaching her what he could. She was better than her brother had indicated, but then George was a better fencer than he. Her lithe little body moved with the grace of a ballet dancer and sweat broke out on his forehead every time he made a touch. He began to correct her movements in a dry, detached voice, and she attempted to disengage more neatly. His longer arm length was counteracted by her lightning speed.

"Try a cutover, Diana," he instructed tersely. "Backward first, then forward." And again, "Use a lateral there," or "Don't slide your toes back." His foil, deflected, touched where her breast was beneath the padded jacket and ridiculous frilled shirt. She gasped and stepped back.

"Have I hurt you?" he demanded when she did not come forward.

"No. A moment, please." She turned her back to him.

He pulled his mask off, leaving his hair rumpled and

damp on his forehead. The tension in his body created by trying to prevent the obvious sign of physical arousal kept him frozen.

"Has the button come off your foil?" she asked, her back still to him but her mask off now.

Dazed, he regarded the foil held limply in his hand and groaned. "Yes. It must just have happened or I would have noticed it." Or maybe I wouldn't have, he thought furiously. I cannot *think*. "I *did* hurt you, didn't I?" he exclaimed angrily as he strode over to her and, catching her by the shoulders, turned her around to face him.

There were tears in her eyes and a spot of blood on the jacket. "Oh my God," he moaned.

"It is nothing. I was surprised."

Alma pulled the jacket from her tiny frame and threw it on the floor. The frilled shirt had a slightly larger stain but it was not spreading. He whipped a handkerchief from his pocket and, handing it to her, turned his back. She turned away also and unbuttoned the shirt and lifted her chemise to inspect the injury. It was a small cut, no longer bleeding, high on her left breast. She used his handkerchief first to angrily wipe away her tears and then to rub away the blood. When she had pulled down the chemise and buttoned the shirt she spoke. "It is only a scratch, Alma, nothing to concern you." When he did not turn she went to him and placed her fingers on his arm.

He turned then and she saw the anguish on his face. "Truly, it is nothing."

"Oh, Diana, forgive me. I didn't notice the button had come off."

"I know that. I have made a fuss about nothing," she said sheepishly, and hung her head.

Alma put his arms around her and hugged her to him, the desire to do so now so strong that he could not resist it. She did not struggle and he attempted to make the gesture seem natural by saying gruffly, "I didn't mean to frighten you, Diana."

When she lifted her face to look at him, the hazel eyes soft and luminous, he automatically leaned down to kiss the parted lips. His kiss was returned with a degree of passion that startled him and made him lose the remnants of caution remaining to him. He pressed her body against his and felt her hands encircle his waist. All the while he kissed her, his head bent to meet the face so far below him, his hands wandered gently over her body, down her back and over her firm little buttocks in the tight breeches. He lifted her in his arms and seated the two of them on the floor. When he touched her breasts she opened her eyes, but he could not read the expression in them. He began to unbutton the frilled shirt, but with a determined though not angry movement she stayed his hands, rose to her feet, and walked the length of the gallery without a backward glance.

The realization of what he had done descended on him the moment she was out of sight. Dear God, he was losing his mind! To try to seduce a young woman of quality, a virgin, in an extremely accessible room of her own home! Anyone might have walked in. And what the hell did it matter *where* he had tried to do it anyway, he berated himself. He should not have tried to do it anywhere! Damnit, from the moment he had ridden up to the Park he had acted as though he were totally uncivilized —churlish, rude, complaining, and now lecherous. There was no excuse for his behavior. What had come over him? Just two weeks ago he had been a normal member of polite society, living by its rules and enjoying its opportunities. He finished putting away the fencing equipment, bemused by the stain on the padded jacket.

There was nothing for it, he must speak with George. In the event this proved easier than he had thought, for he found his host alone in his library. George glanced up with a lazy smile. "Sorry to have neglected you, Ellis. I trust you have kept amused."

Alma blanched at his words. "I . . . I don't know exactly where to begin, George." He drew a breath and tried to still his turbulent thoughts. "I just tried to seduce your sister."

George regarded him calmly and said, "Sit down, Ellis. Were you fencing with her?"

"What the hell does that have to do with it? Yes, I was."

"I warned you about her fencing outfit, Ellis."

"Well, for God's sake, George, don't you *care?*"

"You said you *tried* to seduce her. I presume you were not successful."

"No, by God, but I might have been!" his friend roared.

"Precisely. Diana might have allowed you to seduce her. Consider the significance of that."

"Are you saying that she is not a virgin?" Alma asked incredulously.

"No, I am reasonably sure she is a virgin. Who stopped it?"

"She did. Do you understand what I'm saying, George? I am losing my mind! I try to seduce your sister and you sit there calmly asking me what happened. I think your whole household is tainted with madness and I have caught it," his friend groaned.

"I doubt it, Ellis, though you have certainly behaved strangely ever since you arrived. The point I was trying to make was that you cannot hold yourself entirely to blame. Diana has a little trouble controlling her . . . desire once it is aroused. She is aware of the problem."

"Aware of the problem! You talk as though she were some kind of wanton," Alma protested angrily.

"Well," George replied with a laugh, "she is wont to consider herself Incorrigibly Loose. I have tried to convince her that there is nothing the matter with her, but she will not believe me."

"George," Alma said patiently, "I have seen her keep that Dodge fellow at a distance and when Edwards tried to kiss her I think she bit him." He smiled for the first time during the interview. "In any case, she jumped out of his phaeton and limped home rather than allow him any privileges."

"She is not attracted to everyone. Walter, she says, is a dull stick, and Frank she thoroughly dislikes. In fact the whole problem arose out of an incident when she was just eighteen, when she was attracted to Mrs. Lewis' nephew Harry and she cannot believe that she has gained the maturity to control herself even now. I am glad to hear that she stopped you, but she will probably be miserable that she allowed you to . . . do whatever you did."

"I will marry her if you think I should, George," Alma offered unhappily.

"Don't be a fool!" George snapped, angry for the first time during the interview. "What in the hell would she do with a husband like you? Be sure, Ellis, that when and if she marries she will marry someone who loves her, accepts her for who she is and wishes to care for her, to say nothing of his being someone *she* loves."

"You do not think that she loves me, perhaps, considering what happened?" Alma asked hesitantly.

"No, I do not. Damnit, Ellis, you should know the difference between desire and love. You and I can satisfy our desire anytime we wish with a little planning. Women do not have that option. And I will not enter into a debate with you as to whether women experience desire, or whether they should," he concluded coldly at his friend's incredulous expression.

"I had no intention of debating you on the matter," Alma replied stiffly. "I am no authority on the subject."

"Do you think you can control yourself around Diana in future?" George asked mildly.

"There will be no need," Alma replied, stung. "I had already informed her that I intend to leave in the morning. I will leave now if you wish."

George tapped his desk with impatient fingers. "Ellis, I have told you that you are only partially to blame, and I do not wish to see you leave in a huff." He paused for a moment and then went on more calmly, "Why do you suppose Diana dresses as she does? It is not because she is ignorant of her looks or of fashion. It is her own way of avoiding overtures from men and reducing temptation. You saw what happened when she dressed for the Dodges' party. She could have a swarm of men at her feet every day if she wished it, but she has this fear that she will not . . . never mind. It is nothing to do with you and I should go to her." George rose to conclude the interview.

"The button came off my foil unnoticed, George, and I accidentally pinked her. She said it was merely a scratch but you might have her maid look at it."

George nodded and put out his hand. "Thank you for coming to me, Ellis. I regret your stay here has been so fraught with disaster."

Alma grasped his hand firmly. "I'm sorry I've been such a troublesome guest. I hope it will not mar our friendship."

"Of course not. I'll see you later."

When George knocked at his sister's door she did not answer. He called to her and she bade him enter. Diana rose from her bed, still in the fencing outfit, and stood with downcast head. George went to the basin and dampened a cloth for her to clean away the tear stains. "This is the second time I have found you crying since I've been home, Diana. It is not like you."

She sighed and seated herself on the bed as he took a chair near it. "Did Alma come to you?"

"Yes, he was upset at his behavior."

"It was not his fault."

"Of course it was his fault, Diana, though I could wish you had not worn your fencing outfit with him. Men are not used to seeing young women dressed so." He indicated the bloodstain on the shirt. "How deeply did he cut you?"

"Barely more than a scratch. It stopped bleeding almost immediately."

"Do you want to talk about what happened?"

Diana moistened her lips and said, "I stopped him after a while, George. He may have told you. But then, we were in the Long Gallery which is not a very private place."

"If you had been intent on satisfying your desire you know a dozen places in the house where you would not have been disturbed," he pointed out.

"I suppose that is true, but I didn't think of it."

"You would have thought of it if you had been unable to control yourself," he assured her.

"Do you think so?"

"Absolutely. Diana, I wish you could forget what

happened when you were so young, and did not clearly understand the implications."

"How can I when something like this happens?" she cried.

"Tell me, did you attempt to attract Ellis' advances?"

"No, of course not. I did not really think about the fencing outfit, George. I am used to wearing it when you and I fence."

"Leave that for now, and consider this. You have spent a great deal of time in his company the last two weeks. He is an attractive man and recently you have been getting along well together. Also, Diana, you must remember that you have seen him naked."

"I know," she whispered, a blush staining her cheeks. "But it was not that, George. When he held me and kissed me and touched me I did not want to think about anything else. I did not *care*, George."

"You must have cared, my dear, for you stopped him."

"Do you know why I stopped him?" When he shook his head she said firmly, "Because I knew he would not be able to live with himself afterwards if I did not."

George smiled tenderly at her and said, "The point is, love, that you were able to stop. Do you think another time there would be no reason? There will always be one, Diana, unless you are married. Nothing like this has happened since the day we talked has it?" he asked curiously.

"No, but then I have not been particularly attracted to anyone since then, George."

"And you are attracted to Ellis?"

"Well, I did not think about it until he held me. So you see, it might have been anyone, might it not?"

"No," he sighed, "I do not think so. It is unfortunate that he allowed himself to be carried away, but you have learned, Diana, that you have control over the situation. Please remember that." George started to rise and stopped. "You know, you might speak with Alonna just to get another woman's point of view. You have not had much female advice on the subject."

"*I* can never get any women to talk about it," Diana said bitterly. "Whenever I try to approach the matter I get only self-righteous platitudes from other virgins who have never even been tempted!"

"The problem is that you have been tempted several times, and most young women are never put in a situation where they are."

"Yes, and when I wear my dowdy clothes you pinch at me to dress more attractively," she flung at him.

"Were you dressed attractively the other day when Frank Edwards tried to kiss you?"

"Oh, Frank! He is just stupidly persistent. How did you know about Frank?"

"Ellis saw it from his bedroom window, I gather."

"It probably gave him ideas," she retorted with a brief show of her mischievous smile.

"That's better. Forget it, love, and talk to Alonna."

chapter fourteen

George was much more disturbed by the occurrence than he allowed either of its participants to suspect. And it was not the attempted seduction which bothered him most, though he wished Ellis had been more in control of himself. George himself had no fear that his sister would find in any such situation the self-control she needed. No, what bothered him were the two participants themselves. Neither of them had come to realize it yet, but in some strange way they had fallen in love. Their relationship had been too stormy and irregular for them to come to an understanding of this, and he was more than willing to throw dust in their eyes, as he had done in the two interviews.

The largest problem was that Ellis was unlikely to accept his own emotions in the matter. Ellis had come through the two weeks bewildered by the fluctuations in his temper and emotions. George regretted allowing Diana to take the arrow out of his friend because it had caused Ellis an embarrassment which exhibited itself in strange ways, and had reflected in his attitude toward Diana. Ellis had finally accustomed himself to thinking of her as a younger brother—George had heard him speak so to her more than once—and even today's events would not likely disillusion him. George felt sure Ellis would go to London and attempt to put the whole two weeks out of his mind forever, and he might be successful.

So there was no use allowing Diana to understand that she had fallen in love with him, because it would only cause her pain. George considered asking Alonna to take Diana with her to Trafford Hall when she returned there, while he went to London to see her father. Diana probably would not wish to go, but most of her neighborhood friends were now in London, and she would be left to brood alone at the Park. With a sigh George straightened his cravat and went in search of his fiancée.

Diana remained in her room until almost dinner time. It was not that she *could* not face Alma, she told herself, but that she would *rather* not. She was annoyed at both of them for their performance in the Long Gallery; at him because he should not have tempted her, at herself because she had been so easy to tempt. Still, as George had pointed out, she had called a halt to it.

Lying on her bed staring at the ceiling she remembered the start of the whole problem. Her governess, Miss Parston, had been the only female to guide her, and Miss Parston had been very reticent on relations between the sexes. She was a kindly woman but offered little advice to her beautiful young charge other than to keep a distance from men. Since this attitude seemed rather ridiculous when George was her best friend, Diana had relegated it to the corner she privately called "Miss Parston's Oddities."

Miss Parston had stayed with her until she was almost eighteen, and George had planned to keep her on as Diana's companion, but the governess's mother had become ill and Miss Parston had gone to her and had not returned. It was during the period when Diana had no one guiding her behavior that Mrs. Lewis's nephew had come to stay with her and had become attached to Diana. He was as young as she with no sense of responsibility and very little sense of propriety. They had begun by meeting while out riding and Diana had thought herself in love with him. It seemed the most natural thing in the world for him to kiss her.

Since there was no one to keep track of her movements, George having gone to London to see if he could find a companion for her, they began to meet each afternoon in the woods to talk and embrace. Diana suspected that this was not proper behavior for a young woman, but she enjoyed it and there was no one to censure her. On the day before her eighteenth birthday Harry brought her a present, a tortoise-shell comb for her hair. She was delighted with it and kissed him warmly in thanks. They were lying on the pine needles in the sun, the sweet aroma surrounding them.

Harry had begun to run his hands over her body, something which she was sure she should not allow, but when she had protested he had reminded her that he loved her—had he not just given her a beautiful comb? He had continued to caress her breasts while he murmured endearments. The warmth which sprang up in her body clouded her mind and she did not protest when he took off her bodice and kissed her breasts. She *knew* that she should not allow him such freedom with her person but her body had begun to ache with desire and she felt powerless to say him nay. He had lifted her skirts and petticoats and begun to stroke her thighs and she felt her breath coming faster. He was struggling to unfasten his pants when George came on the scene.

Returning for her birthday, George had found it suspicious that her horse was tied at the edge of the wood with another one. He did not know Harry and never got to know him. When he came upon them in their compromising position his eyes blazed with fury and he dragged Harry up by his collar and slapped him so hard that the young man fell to his knees. "If you were not so young, I would kill you for this. Never let me set eyes on you again," he roared. Harry took to his heels and left Linton that same afternoon.

Her cheeks flaming with shame, fear and mortification, Diana had tossed down her skirts and clutched her bodice to her chest. Her brother, shaken out of his usual calm, snapped at her to dress herself and meet him in his library. By the time Diana arrived there she was shaking and incoherent. George had recovered some of his usual equanimity by pointing out to himself that he had arrived before she had lost her virginity, unless this was not the first time such a scene had taken place. He felt in no small way to blame for his negligent care of her and seated her gently, providing her with a glass of brandy to restore her color.

"Who was that young man?"

"Mrs. Lewis's nephew Harry."

"Is this the first time something like this has taken place? You must be honest with me, Diana. I will not punish you."

"I promise you it is, George, though he has kissed me before."

"How long have you known him?"

"Two or three weeks."

George drew a hand through his hair. "Diana, do you understand what you were about to do?"

"Well, yes, I think so." Her face had become fiery red.

"Tell me."

"We . . . were . . . about to . . ."

"You were about to mate, Diana. Have you not been told that young girls do not behave in such a fashion?"

"I suppose so."

George attempted to keep the exasperation out of his voice. "You have seen animals mate, Diana. To what purpose do they do so?"

"To have babies," she whispered.

"Precisely. Have you a desire to have a baby out of wedlock?"

"No, George, I did not think of it."

"I want you to do so now, Diana. I also want you to understand that when a man marries you he will expect you to be a virgin; that is, a woman who has not previously mated."

"Do men not mate before they are wed?" she asked innocently.

"Damnit, Diana, we are not talking about men."

"I see," she replied coldly.

He shook his head aggravatedly. "All right, my dear, we will talk about men, too. Yes, most men mate before marriage."

"Then how is it that there are un-mated women left to be married?" she asked with interest.

"Virgins, Diana. Well, men mate with women who . . . have already lost their virginity."

"Married women?"

Distracted, George ran his hand through his hair again. "How have you reached the age of eighteen without learning any of this?" he asked peevishly.

"Who was there to tell me?" she retorted and lifted her chin defensively. "If you do not wish to tell me you need not."

"I am going to tell you," he grumbled. "Obviously

you need to know. You are of gentle birth, and you are expected to live by the rules which govern our particular group of people. One of those rules is that you do not mate until you are wed, and you mate only with your husband once you are wed. There are those even in the highest levels of society who do not live by those rules, and they are sometimes condoned; but I should never like to see you be one of them. In exchange for the privileges you receive because you are of gentle birth, the respect you command, you must endeavor to live by the rules laid down for you."

"You still have not explained whom men mate with," she reminded him.

"I am coming to that," he replied with asperity. "There are some women, almost never of gentle birth, who do not live by the same rules as we do."

"How convenient for men!"

"Diana," he said threateningly, "I want you to listen without another word. These women make their living by selling their bodies to men. It is not a pleasant life, as you can imagine, and often is embarked on without a real appreciation of the consequences. Can you understand that?"

"Yes, I suppose so, but, George, I cannot see why a man would pay a woman when he could marry someone and . . ."

"Not every man wishes to marry."

"Then perhaps he should not mate," Diana suggested stubbornly.

"Today when you were in the woods, did you know that you should not be intimate with Harry?"

"Yes."

"Then why were you about to?"

"Because I . . ."

"Precisely. You felt a desire to do so. Well, men often feel that desire, and as we live by the rules which forbid us to mate with unmarried women of quality we satisfy our desires in the only honorable channel."

"It does not sound so very honorable to me. And what of women who desire to mate? What do they do?"

"Nothing, until they are married."

"How very unfair!"

"Yes, it is, Diana, but there is no help for it. I should hate to see you with child and unmarried. You would be ruined. It is not a matter taken lightly by society, nor ever forgiven."

"I see."

"I do not know how it is with women, Diana," he said apologetically. "Since most manage to enter marriage as virgins I have always suspected that their desire is perhaps not so general as men's, but I cannot be sure. It may be that a woman's desire is not inflamed except by actual contact with a man. If that is the case then the rules which say you shall not have any intimate contact with men before marriage make some sense. Ordinarily you could rely on a young man of your station not to impose himself on you. Your friend Harry was an exception, perhaps too young to understand the gravity of his offense. You are not to see him again, Diana."

"But I am very fond of him," she pleaded.

"Do you think you could trust him to behave himself properly?"

Diana did not answer.

"Then you must not see him again, my love, for it would be sure to lead to trouble."

A lone tear rolled down her cheek.

"I would not forbid it if it were not so very important, Diana," he said sympathetically. "But your friend is not someone you would wish to marry if he would treat you so. Please believe me. In time you will feel better."

And in time she had. Harry had left the area and Diana spent more time with her other friends. She had tried to discuss with the young women their own feelings of desire, but they shunned such discussions and as often as not had no idea what she meant. Diana had begun to feel an oddity, the only woman she knew who experienced this desire. There were any number of men who were attracted to her; but she was not attracted to them, and they never went beyond mere dallying. Nevertheless, she started to dress less attractively except for special occasions, and the young men were not such a nuisance.

Walter Dodge, virtuous as he was, courted her because he thought her goodness was worthy of him, and it did no harm that she was beautiful as well. Frank Edwards thought her a gem of the first order and had a burning desire to exhibit such a prize catch in London, where she was practically unknown. Diana had not experienced desire with either of these two men, in fact, had only experienced it in a general way in the years since Harry. She had learned to deal with her own needs, something she had never discussed with George, of course; but she was content with her life and her pursuits.

It was therefore with a great deal more surprise than her brother suspected that she had succumbed to passion in Alma's arms. Their turbulent acquaintance had not prepared her for her reaction when he held her. And in spite of what she had said to George, she had indeed learned that she was now in control of herself, if only because she would never shame her brother so. The memory of George's words had been with her, and she had thought of Alma's shame if he allowed himself to conclude what he had started. Somehow she knew too, even if Alma did not, that he would not have. For all his cantankerous behavior there was a hard core of decency about him which would have brought him up short of taking her virginity.

Diana sighed and rose to dress for dinner. She should never have insisted on removing the arrow. That was at the root of all their problems, she suspected. She had shamed Alma and today's events were an attempt, though unconscious probably, to prove his power over her, to show that his masculinity was dominant in spite of all her petty tyrannies.

The five people who sat down to dinner that evening were rather subdued. Mrs. Lewis had learned that Lord Alma was leaving and she supposed that she would no longer be needed at the Park. George had told Alonna only that there was a bit of tension between Alma and Diana again, and the two themselves were enough to make even George cringe. Alma treated Diana with the deference he might have shown his own grandmother, and Diana acted as though she were. It would have been very amusing to George if it had not been so pathetic. Their performance continued through the evening, even to the songs they chose to sing, lugubrious numbers with no life to them. George felt a profound sense of relief when Diana announced that she was going to bed.

She was tempted to stay in bed the next morning and allow Alma to leave without her saying good-bye, but she did not do so. She and George and Alonna were there to see him climb into his carriage. With due gravity, Alma thanked Diana for her attention to him during his stay, and she responded that it had been her pleasure.

When the carriage with Crusader tied behind was out of sight she had her mare saddled and took a long ride. On her return George invited her to come with him to Trafford Hall, where he would stay for a few days before heading for London to speak with Alonna's father.

"I thought you might like to stay on at the Hall with me," Alonna suggested, "since most of your friends are not here. George will only be there a few days."

Diana considered the possibility and at length agreed to it, for George would not stay long in London, but would wish to return to the Park to set things in motion for its new mistress. When George had left them alone Diana and Alonna discussed the changes George had suggested in the suite which would be his wife's.

"George has told you that I intend to move to the Dower House, has he not?" Diana asked.

"Why should you do that? There is plenty of room here, certainly," Alonna protested.

"Yes, I know, but I have always thought that a newly married couple should have their house to themselves. I shall not mind, you know. I rode over to the Dower House the other day to inspect it. It has not been occupied in years and I have an itch to start work on it."

"But this is your home, and has been all your life."

"Then it's high time I made a change," Diana replied with a grin.

"I wish you would not," Alonna said sadly. "I shall feel as though I have driven you out."

"Don't be a goose!" Diana hugged the younger woman. "I shall be here more than you wish, no doubt."

"No, I shall be happy to have you around any time . . . well, almost any time," Alonna confessed with a blush.

"Alonna, George suggested I speak with you about the desire women feel for men, but I do not wish to embarrass you. When I have tried to talk with my friends they do not seem to wish to speak of it."

"I'm sure I would have found the same, my dear, but I have several sisters who have been married for some years and they did not wish me to be so innocent as they had been, so we have discussed it often. I was shy about it at first but they persisted, telling me that the more I understood about physical relations between men and women the more I would be able to cope with men and eventually marriage."

"Do you think it's natural for a woman to experience desire for a man sometimes?" Diana asked hesitantly.

"I hope so," Alonna laughed. "My sisters married men they loved and they are not ashamed to admit that they feel desire for their husbands. I had not understood so well until I met George."

"But you have never felt desire for someone you did not love?" Diana asked.

Alonna's eyes twinkled. "I would not say that. I have met some very charming rascals who were . . . exciting."

Diana heaved a sigh of relief and smiled at her friend. "Yes, I suppose that is true. I'm glad we talked, Alonna."

Their stay at Trafford Park was more pleasurable than Diana had expected. George was welcomed by his old acquaintances and she herself was adopted by them into a round of morning calls and dinner parties. Although George had insisted that she dress her best for their stay, Diana was not reluctant. The announcement of Alonna's engagement to Vallert had not been retracted, as that young man had refused to be intimidated by her threat. Since George was eager to set the matter straight, and to receive Lord Franston's permission to wed his daughter, he suggested after a few days that he should leave for London.

Margaret had considered the possibility of her father being stubborn and said, "I think you should go with him, Alonna. I feel sure Papa will not refuse his permission if you are there."

"I do not expect any trouble with Papa," Alonna retorted. "I am sure one man is just as well as another to him so long as I am safely married off soon."

"No doubt, but I think it would be wisest. You have never been seen with Vallert since the announcement, and it will lend credit to your version of the matter if you are seen with George."

"True. Do you wish me to come, George?" she asked, turning to him.

George had been leaning against the mantelpiece listening to their discussion and it had suggested an idea to him. "Yes, I think it would be wise. I should like Diana to come, too."

Diana turned a startled gaze to her brother. "Me? Why ever do you want me to come?"

"For several reasons, my dear. Many of your friends are there already. It will be sadly dull at the Park right now, and you will need to choose some clothes for my wedding," he reminded her glibly.

"Do come, Diana," Alonna urged. "London is quite active at this time of year and we can go to the theatre and to balls and ride in the park." Alonna hugged her friend and whispered in her ear, "I could use your support, love. Please say you will come."

A strange mixture of emotions had engulfed Diana when George suggested that she accompany them. Her natural reluctance to face the stilted style of society was tempered by a strong desire to indulge in the sophisticated pastimes just this once. Her freedom at the Park was all very well and entertaining, but she was curious to see another way of life, one which both George and Alonna, not such very different people than she, seemed to enjoy wholeheartedly. She no longer really feared that she was Incorrigibly Loose, either, and her previous refusal had been largely based on that premise and maintained willy-nilly in the face of any contrary evidence. But Alma would be there, and she was not sure she wanted to see him. "Very well, I should like to come," she agreed.

chapter fifteen

After conveying Alonna to her father's, and leaving word that he wished to speak with Lord Franston, George settled his sister in his town house. Diana had seldom been in London and then for only a few days each time, and she agreed to take her maid with her to the modiste George recommended while he settled his business.

Lord Franston had been browbeaten by his daughter into accepting an interview with George, and was in no good humor when the younger man arrived. Franston waved him carelessly to a well-worn leather chair and seated himself impatiently at his desk.

"I have come to ask your permission to wed your daughter," George said politely.

"So she says," Franston grumbled. "Seems to make no difference to her that she is already engaged to Vallert."

"I think you are well aware that she never consented to marry Vallert, Lord Franston. I am surprised that you did not have the announcement refuted."

"No reason she should not marry him. Perfectly good fellow."

"But she does not wish to marry him, and it is inconceivable to me that you can call a man who falsely announces his engagement a perfectly good fellow."

"I had given him my permission to marry her."

"It is customary to have the woman's permission as well."

"It will cause a great to-do to change things now," the old man muttered.

"I think you can safely leave that to me, sir. Do I have your permission to marry Alonna?"

"Vallert has a title," Franston said slyly.

George refused to give him the satisfaction of informing him that one day in the future, when his recluse bachelor uncle died, he also would have a title. "It does not seem to have won him any influence with your daughter."

"I won't force her to marry him," Franston conceded grudgingly.

"I am pleased to hear it. We had in mind to wed in two months time, sir, and I should like to announce our engagement now."

"Oh, very well. If she wishes to wed you I will not stand in the way, but see that there is no scandal, Savile. Vallert is a hot-tempered fellow, very unpredictable."

"I appreciate your caution, Lord Franston." George rose from his chair and offered his hand to his prospective father-in-law, who shook it unenthusiastically.

"Take care of her. She's not a bad chit," Franston mumbled.

"I shall do my best," George promised.

Alonna was awaiting her fiancé in a small room off the hall and George went to assure her that all was well. She regarded him quizzingly and asked, "He did not raise a fuss?"

"Very little. He told me to take care of you."

"Did he?" Alonna's eyes softened. "That was kind of him."

"Very proper," George agreed solemnly as he kissed her. "I must see Vallert now. Your father does not wish any to-do."

"Nor do I, George. Do not let Vallert embroil you," she pleaded gravely.

"Trust me, love," he grinned.

"I wish you would be serious."

"I am serious," he protested as he kissed her nose.

She sighed, despairing of impressing him with the importance of his mission. "Will I see you later?"

"I hope you will join my sister and me for the theatre, Miss Sanfield."

"I should be delighted, Mr. Savile."

"Excellent. Until later, my dear."

Lord Vallert's lodgings were in James Street and George had the good fortune to find his lordship at home.

Each day Vallert had checked the papers, with a

growing confidence as no retraction appeared. He was smug in facing Alonna's other suitor. "To what do I owe the honor of this visit, Savile?"

"I wanted you to be one of the first to hear of my engagement," George replied blithely.

"No, really? To whom have you become engaged?"

"To Miss Alonna Sanfield."

Vallert's face darkened dangerously and he rasped. "Your jest is not in good taste, Savile. You must be aware that I am engaged to Miss Sanfield."

"She does not seem to agree with you, for she has consented to be my wife, and her father has obligingly granted his permission."

"I shall call you out for this!"

"No, I don't think so. I have undertaken to handle the matter with as little fuss as possible, and I cannot consider a duel as unattended by notoriety."

When Vallert made to strike him in the usual manner of a challenge, George caught his hand in a grip of steel. "You have no one but yourself to blame for the mess you're in, Vallert. You have caused Miss Sanfield a great deal of distress, for which I find it very difficult to forgive you. In an effort to see the matter amicably settled, however, I am willing to offer you some assistance. The day after tomorrow the announcement of our engagement will appear. I suggest that you attend the theatre with Miss Sanfield, my sister and myself this evening."

"You are mad!"

"Hardly. I am offering you a way to save face, you young gudgeon. If you are seen to be on satisfactory terms with us it will not be so difficult for you. A misunderstanding; Miss Sanfield's affections were previously engaged. If you persist in your perfidy I shall have no recourse but to expose you, which I am not in the least loath to do."

"You wouldn't dare," Vallert blurted uncertainly.

George's eyes blazed for a moment before he replied calmly. "It is your privilege to wait and see, Vallert, but the results will not be to your liking. In the end I shall wed Miss Sanfield. Do you go to the theatre with us?"

Vallert clenched his hands at his sides but replied, "Very well, Savile."

Their group at the theatre caused no little comment. George made it perfectly clear that he was with Alonna, who had not been overly enthusiastic about including Vallert in their party but agreed that it was perhaps a wise move. The burden of Vallert's presence, however, rested on Diana and she was predisposed to dislike him. He did nothing to disillusion her but rather reminded her disagreeably of Frank Edwards, who arrived at their box during the first intermission amidst expressions of astonishment at seeing Diana in town. She denied him leave to call on her, which merely made him sulk, but did not make him leave the box. When the second act was about to begin, George finally sent him away.

Vallert, intrigued by Diana's beauty and her handling of her suitor, began to make an effort to attract her, which was more disagreeable to her than his previous sullenness. She remained distantly polite and welcomed the arrival of the Dodges and Barsetts at the second intermission. There was barely time to greet them before George's friend Cranmer arrived to be presented to Diana, whom he had noticed from his box across the way. Considering the amount of chatter in the box sufficient cover for his remark, he said to George, "You cannot seriously expect me to believe that your sister shot Ellis with an arrow." His eyes rested admiringly on Diana; Cranmer was a connoisseur.

Mockingly, George agreed that it was highly improbable, and rewarded his friend by introducing him to his sister. Diana had not heard the remark and greeted him politely. Cranmer murmured conversationally, "I understand you are interested in archery, Miss Savile."

"I am interested in many things, Mr. Cranmer," she replied, her eyes twinkling.

"So am I. We must discuss them sometime. May I call on you tomorrow?" He was laughing at her, but not unkindly, and she agreed.

When the box had cleared for the third act Diana happened to glance down and she saw Alma seated with a beautiful young woman who was very elegantly dressed.

Diana immediately turned her eyes to the stage, since she had no desire to exchange nods with him, or to be thought interested in his presence. She did not glance in his direction again.

Several days previously Lord Alma had arrived in London tired and sore. He determinedly put the events of the previous two weeks out of his mind and reverted to his normal good-natured, gallant behavior. There were several invitations in the stack of cards awaiting his attention which he set aside as being of interest, the others he dismissed. He took four letters with him when he went to his study and read them at his leisure while he sipped at a glass of wine, standing up. The hours in the carriage had been aggravatingly painful in spite of frequent stops.

Two of the letters bore the same handwriting, and he remembered, with a grimace, telling George politely that he had no pressing engagements in London. Fanny's first letter was a cheerful greeting; she expected to see him any day now. Her second letter was a trifle testy, he thought with amusement. It was really too late then to do anything about it, but he scribbled an explanation and a request to call on her, and handed it to a footman to be delivered the next morning.

There was a reply on the tray with the silver chocolate pot when he awoke in the morning. Fanny considered it most unlikely that she would forgive him, but he might try to convince her if he called at three. Alma smiled as he sipped at his chocolate. There were many advantages to a woman such as Fanny, who maintained her own house and was very selective in her clients. She had been bequeathed a staggering sum on the death of an admiring elderly gentleman, and she was more pleasure-loving than greedy. Not that her companionship was given without cost (she had a respectable opinion of her worth); but she was not forever beseeching one for a new gown or a necklace. Her services came with a fixed price, no extras. Alma presented himself, impeccably dressed, at three.

Fanny received him in her parlor. "You are looking

very well, Ellis . . . for someone who has been laid up in the country for two weeks with an injury."

Alma grasped her hands and kissed each in turn. His eyes mischievous he said, "I shall show you my wound if you like."

"I have a feeling you would be only too happy to do so," she retorted as she patted the seat beside her on the sofa.

He seated himself, thought better of taking her in his arms immediately, and replied, "Yes, it is in a most intriguing spot. I assure you, lovely Fanny, that I only arrived in London last evening and wrote you first thing. I slept with your letters next my heart," he added soulfully.

"So flattering," she mocked. "Your wound must not be near your heart."

"No, no, I assure you it is not. Shall I show it to you?" he asked eagerly, his eyes dancing.

"No, naughty boy, you shall not. I have not decided yet to forgive you."

"How may I convince you, my dear? Shall I beg you on my knees or fight a duel for you?" He gave convincing demonstrations of his skills in both.

Fanny was entertained by his high spirits and evident delight in being with her again. She held out a hand to him where he stood mock-penitent before her and he pulled her into his arms. His kiss and the evidence of his passion were so obvious that when he picked her up in his arms she laughed and said, "You have been without for some time, Ellis."

"I do not deny it," he grinned, as he strode with her to her bedchamber.

It was some time before Fanny had a chance to remark on his scar. "Whatever did you do to yourself?" she asked incredulously.

"One of my friends has a sister who is, so she tells me, the acknowledged woman archer of Cambridgeshire. She shot me."

Fanny giggled. "Were you misbehaving, Ellis?"

"Not then," he grunted. "I don't want to talk about it."

"Well, it is a lovely scar," she conceded as she toyed with the wrinkled skin. Alma grasped her waist and rolled over on her as she squealed, "Already?" It was several hours before Alma left, finally satiated. "You could wear a woman out," Fanny scolded as he kissed her on leaving.

Alma thoroughly enjoyed being back in London. He took care of several business matters, attended a number of balls, flirted with various young women, rode in the park, gambled, and took advantage of what the town had to offer. Generally he spent a great deal of his time at Stillings or travelling, but he enjoyed London when he was there.

No day went past that he did not visit Fanny. There was a good amount of time to make up for and he intended to relish every moment of it. Fanny was accommodating to his whims as a rule, but she refused to don breeches for him. "They are most unfeminine, Ellis, and I will not put them on. I have the most delightful confection, all in sheer gold, that you will adore." Alma agreed that it was delightful.

The evening that he took her to the theatre he was horrified to see Diana in a box with her brother and his two other guests. Alma made no attempt to attract their attention or to visit their box, but Fanny noticed his glances in their direction and asked who they were.

"One of them is the archer," he replied briefly.

"The blond or the brunette?"

"The brunette."

"She looks too small to lift a bow, let alone shoot you with an arrow that would make such a scar."

"She was using a hunting arrow."

"Well, I should thank her for leaving such a delightful mark upon you," Fanny giggled.

"I am sure she does not regret it in the least," Alma replied bitterly. "I could not sit or lie on my back for the better part of two weeks, Fanny. You have no idea how inconvenient that is."

"*I* would find it impossible," his companion retorted with a throaty chuckle.

Cranmer arrived at Alma's the day after meeting Diana at the theatre. It had occurred to him that it would be great sport to take Alma along when he paid his call on the diminutive beauty.

"I don't wish to see her," Alma replied in answer to the suggestion.

"You really should go, you know. It would not be polite to avoid her after being her guest for so long."

"I was her brother's guest. Has George fixed everything right and tight with Lord Franston?"

"Yes, they are to wed in two months. He took Vallert with him last night to help the young nodcock save face, I dare say. More than I would have done."

"I doubt Vallert will appreciate the effort," Alma retorted scornfully.

"But it may save a deal of scandal for them all. Really, Ellis, you should come with me."

"Well, I won't," Alma said stubbornly.

Cranmer shrugged. "As you wish."

He found Diana entertaining all of the people who had been in the box the previous evening. Having been introduced to Allison and Walter Dodge at that time, he now spent a few moments speaking with them. Carson Barsett he knew, but Jenette was a newcomer to London and likely to be much in demand, so he made an effort to charm her. Vallert he acknowledged but did not speak with. When all the others took their leave except George and Alonna, he finally had a chance to have a few words with Diana.

"I see you do not intend to lead a quiet life in London this visit, Miss Savile. George has never before even introduced you to me when you've been here."

"I have seldom stayed for more than a few days, Mr. Cranmer, but then George has never before been engaged."

"I'm pleased everything worked out for him. Do you stay long this visit?"

"I hardly know. Do you live in London, Mr. Cranmer?"

"Yes, for the most part. It is tiresome to journey to Yorkshire very often," he replied lazily.

"Ah, yes, very tiresome," she agreed with mock sympathy. "Do you not long to see the countryside? To ride wherever you wish? To hunt and fish?"

"I would rather dance with beautiful women and attend the theatre. But if you prefer outdoor diversions may I offer to take you driving in the park this afternoon?" He smiled at her engagingly.

"I would like that, Mr. Cranmer."

He came for her in a dashing phaeton with a pair, one white horse and one black with red plumes. Diana had forgotten how elegantly attired were all those strolling, riding and driving through the park of an afternoon. Cranmer was a charming companion; he had tales of most of the people they passed, and seemed to know everyone. His beaver was constantly tipped, and he occasionally introduced her to someone as George Savile's sister. They had just turned and were heading back toward the gates when they met Lord Alma and the same young woman Diana had seen with him the previous evening. Alma was riding Crusader gingerly and Fanny was mounted on a small chestnut mare.

Although Cranmer should merely have acknowledged them, he had a nose for mischief and could not resist reining in his pair. Diana was tempted to pinch him, but she maintained her poise and smiled kindly at the couple.

Alma seethed inwardly. He had no intention of introducing Fanny to Diana; it was not done. It was unnecessary, however, as Cranmer was acquainted with her and performed the introduction himself. Fanny, looking radiant in a blue riding outfit with silver braid, smiled at Diana and murmured, "So pleased to meet you, Miss Savile." Her eyes were dancing merrily and Alma whispered menacingly, "If you say anything, Fanny, I shall . . ."

But it was Cranmer who blandly commented, "Miss Savile lives in the country, Fanny, and seldom gets to town. She is quite an accomplished archer, I believe," he remarked, turning to his companion for confirmation.

Diana did pinch him then, surreptitiously, and said coldly, "I doubt that Miss Hopkins is interested in archery, Mr. Cranmer."

During this interchange Alma sat his horse rigidly, his face frozen in grim lines. Fanny replied, "Oh, I find archery a fascinating sport. So much more ancient than all these firearms, almost primitive, and surely just as dangerous." Alma abruptly suggested that they should not keep their horses standing and politely bid Diana and Cranmer farewell.

"That was very naughty of you, Mr. Cranmer," Diana scolded. "It was obvious from Alma's face that she is not someone I should be introduced to, and I cannot imagine what possessed you to speak of archery."

"I could not resist it," he admitted with a grin.

Diana considered him gravely for a moment. "George told you," she said accusingly. "He should not have."

"No, I suppose not," he replied judiciously. "Still, since he had . . ."

"You thought you would work a little mischief. You may take me directly home, Mr. Cranmer," she said coldly.

Cranmer glanced at the angry little face beside him and said apologetically, "I am sorry, Miss Savile. I thought it amusing that you had shot Alma with an arrow. I see I was wrong." He urged the horses to a better pace and swung out through the gates.

When Diana realized that Cranmer knew no more than he had just said, she supposed it might have seemed amusing to him, but she was not in a mood to overlook the discomfort she had suffered. For his part, Cranmer thought she felt upset about the accident and did his best to cheer her out of her annoyance with him. He was only partially successful, for she was still distantly polite when he helped her to alight from the phaeton. "George has asked me if I would accompany the three of you to the Austin ball this evening," he said hesitantly. "If you would prefer that I do not, you have only to say so."

Ashamed of herself, Diana said sadly, "No, Mr. Cranmer, I would be pleased for your escort. I didn't mean to sulk." She raised her hazel eyes to him and smiled uncertainly. "I hope we will be friends."

"I feel sure we will," he replied sincerely, moved by her frankness. When she had disappeared into the house he promised himself that he would not displease her again if he could avoid it. She was entirely too feisty and too trusting to be taken lightly, and she was George's sister.

chapter sixteen

When Alma and Fanny rode away from the phaeton, he was in a mood to box her ears and did not speak for some time. She was regretting the impulse that had led her to say anything at all, and she eyed Alma through her lashes. Never had she seen his demeanor other than easygoing . . . or passionate. The man riding beside her was angry and withdrawn. When their silence had continued unbearably long she reached out a hand and touched his sleeve. He was tempted to shake off her hand but instead patted it and smiled ruefully. "I know I should not be angry with you, Fanny. It was just a little joke of Cranmer's. I'll wager Di—Miss Savile snapped his nose off for it, too." He laughed at the imagined scene, consequently regaining his good humor. "I cannot be with you this evening, Fanny, so let's go to your house now," he murmured with a lecherous wink. She laughed and agreed.

Alma had reconsidered attending the Austin ball, knowing Diana was in town. He had planned to go, but he was sure to meet her there and he could not feel comfortable with her now. She had been dressed in the most becoming amber dress for her ride with Cranmer, lace at her throat framing the tiny face with its intent hazel eyes. Alma wondered idly if she had read his books. At length he dressed for the ball, determined to ask Miss Savile to stand up for a set early in the evening so that his duty would be done and he could avoid her for the remainder of the evening.

When he arrived he noted with chagrin that she was already surrounded by a number of young men but he patiently joined the circle. He managed to solicit a set well into the evening. Resigned, he stood up with Allison Dodge and then Jenette Barsett. After two further sets with other young ladies of his acquaintance, he adjourned to the card room for a while. Cranmer had just finished a hand of whist and offered Alma his place but Alma refused. He went instead to George, who was speaking with his host. When George was alone Alma said, "I understand Lord Franston has agreed to the match, George. When does the announcement appear?"

"In the morning."

"Have you settled everything with Vallert?"

"I hope so. Hot-tempered young devil."

"He's been buzzing around your sister tonight. Perhaps you should check the papers tomorrow for an announcement of *their* engagement."

"Diana does not like him."

"That did not stop him with Miss Sanfield, as I recall."

George considered him thoughtfully. "I dare say he would not repeat the performance, but I will keep an eye on him. Cranmer says you were with Fanny in the park, and he forced an introduction on Diana. He was apologetic."

"I could have wrung his neck, George. He introduced your sister as being from the country, and a noted archer."

George laughed. "I imagine Fanny found that very amusing."

"Yes, she remarked that she thought it dangerous sport," Alma grumbled, his hand unconsciously touching the spot of his almost healed wound.

"I told Cranmer no more than that Diana had shot you with an arrow, Ellis."

Alma eyed him defiantly. "I wish you had not."

"You take the matter too seriously, Ellis. I wish you could see its comic side."

"Perhaps some day I will," Alma replied grudgingly. "I must get back to the ballroom. Excuse me."

The groups were already forming for the cotillion when he made his way to Diana, who was fending off Vallert. "Forgive me, Miss Savile, I was speaking with your brother in the card room. I believe this is our dance."

"Yes," Diana replied, disgruntled. "I was having a difficult time making Lord Vallert understand that I was already spoken for for the cotillion."

Alma turned to the belligerent Vallert and murmured, "You seem to have a great deal of trouble accepting no as an answer, my lord. Miss Savile shoots people who annoy her."

Vallert stalked away and Diana stared at Alma in amazement. "How could you say such a thing to him?"

"Your brother has advised me to see the comic side of the incident, Miss Savile, and in my heavy-handed way I was trying to do so."

"Well, I did not shoot you because I was annoyed with you. I did not even know you."

"You see, there is all the more reason to warn Vallert," Alma mocked.

Diana gave a gurgle of laughter as they were parted by the movement of the dance. When they were rejoined he asked, "Is George to be wed in town?"

"Yes, Lord Franston is not interested in making the effort to have the wedding at his seat, and Alonna thought it simpler here."

"Do you stay in town long?"

"I'm not sure. I have been enjoying myself this time, so I feel in no hurry to leave."

"Have you done anything with the chariot?"

"No, but I have in mind to write a play centered around it, for Christmastime, you know. I thought to entitle it *The Wounded Warrior*," she replied with an expressionless face.

Alma regarded her suspiciously but made no comment. Diana continued, "It would be the story of a warrior-god come down to earth to offer his magnificent presence to the humble people who worship him. Tragically, on landing in a turnip field with his blazing chariot he stubs his toe."

"Diana . . ." Alma said warningly.

Undaunted, his parner went on blithely, "The villagers make every effort to succor him, balms and potions, even incantations. All their efforts are to no avail. His toe swells to the size of his head and he is unable to walk amongst his admirers."

"Diana . . ."

"Do you not think it a good subject for a play, Alma?" she asked innocently. "But wait, you have not heard all of it yet. The villagers in desperation decide to sacrifice a maiden to this god, in order that his toe may heal."

"Not another word, you wretched girl!"

"I must say you are not encouraging of my artistic genius," she declaimed. "Well, perhaps George will tell you of it some day."

"He had better not."

"So few people are interested in amateur dramatics," she sighed. "Frank Edwards is, you know, though he is intent on acting. Romeo, I think."

"I have noticed."

"I have met several people in London who would do well in the theatre," she mused. "I should like to see Lord Vallert play Iago and Lord Franston as King Lear. Now Cranmer would make an excellent Falstaff, and do you not think perhaps your friend, Miss Hopkins, isn't it, so charming as she is, would be ideal as . . ."

"Spare me, young lady. I should have given you a copy of *Pilgrim's Progress* for your birthday instead of a book on medicinal herbs," Alma said sternly, his eyes dancing. "And you have only been in London two days."

"It is the rarified atmosphere here, I think. One cannot help but be influenced by it. I have taken," she said, dropping her voice to a conspiratorial whisper, "to writing verse."

Alma had no chance to reply to this information because another partner was awaiting Diana. He stood at the side watching her trim little figure move through the steps of the dance, her face smiling up at her partner. At least they were past the discomfort that had followed his rash behavior, he thought with relief. Lord, he would never understand what had come over him, and what was more, he had no intention of trying. There was Fanny now to satisfy any cravings he might have, and he could continue to lead the contented life he was used to. Alma left the ball soon after.

The announcement of the engagement of Alonna Sanfield and George Savile appeared in the papers the next day. Vallert found that, for all his protestations of a misunderstanding and his explanation, he had done the honorable thing when he discovered that Miss Sanfield's affections were previously engaged. He was regarded with a certain amount of incredulity, even mockery, by his acquaintance. He chafed under this ignominy and instead of appreciating George Savile's efforts to help him save face, he began to resent them. Then there was the matter of Savile's sister. Diana Savile had not been accepting of his advances the previous evening, and when he followed a bouquet of flowers with his own presence, he was denied. The more he thought of this insult, the angrier he became. Vallert was not used to having his wishes opposed, for he had been spoiled from childhood by an indulgent mother who still considered him a paragon of every virtue, an opinion he had easily adopted. There was no excuse for first Alonna Sanfield and then Diana Savile to treat him so disrespectfully.

As the days progressed and Vallert saw Diana at various parties and musical evenings his interest in her increased, while hers in him appeared to sustain no improvement. He was encouraged, however, that she evidenced no partiality to anyone. Cranmer usually escorted her along with her brother and Alonna, but Diana showed him merely a friendly gratitude. Vallert had witnessed the distance at which Diana kept Frank Edwards and Walter Dodge; the only person she treated with more than normal courtesy was Lord Alma, who was not often present at these entertainments. Vallert did not like the familiarity between them; but it did not amount to flirtatiousness on either side, so he discarded any attachment in that direction. No, he had a perfectly free field and he intended to use it.

It was a week, however, before Vallert happened to overhear someone mention that Diana frequently rode in the park early in the morning. She would be accompanied by a groom of course, but that did not need to bother him unduly. With his offer to escort her, the groom could be sent home, or diverted.

The morning he chose to carry out his plan happened to follow a ball at which Diana had seen Alma, after an absence of several days. Alma had found himself, much to his surprise, asking her if he might ride with her in the morning, and Diana had agreed to meet him in the park if he wished to ride as early as she did, and he had consented.

When Diana arrived at the park she did not see Alma, but Vallert was riding near the gates and came to join her. He did not think to ask her if he might join her, so she did not bother to tell him that she was to meet Alma. Besides, Alma was nowhere to be seen, and Diana assumed that he had thought better of rising so early after a late night. When they had ridden some distance from the entrance Vallert asked Diana if she would mind if he sent her groom back to the entrance to advise his friend Considine which direction he had taken. Although Diana agreed readily enough, the maneuver put her on her guard. Vallert in a stroke of unknowing genius offered to show her the reservoir, which piqued her curiosity.

They rode through the symmetrical rows of trees and dismounted at the reservoir, where Diana started plying him with questions of water distribution in London. Since Vallert had not the faintest notion how water was distributed in the metropolis and could not believe that any young woman would have the slightest interest in such a matter, he considered this a delaying tactic on her part, due to shyness no doubt. He therefore put his arms around her and began to kiss and fondle her in spite of her protests, which she accompanied by battering against his chest with her small fists. Since he refused to break his hold on her, she brought her knee forcefully up to his groin and he went white with pain.

When Alma arrived at the gates of the park he solicited Diana's direction from her groom, chiding him for a fool for leaving his mistress with the likes of Vallert. The groom had not been able to keep pace with Alma on Crusader and so did not witness Diana's exhibition; Alma did, and he was livid. Diana, unaware of his arrival on the scene, turned and mounted her mare, as she spoke to the helpless Vallert. "I have no wish to be in your company ever again, Lord Vallert. Please do not forget that."

She swung her mare about and saw Alma. "I thought you had overslept, Alma." With a mischievous glance behind her she added, "Lord Vallert has kindly kept me company."

"Don't be absurd, Diana. I saw what happened," he rasped. Jumping down from Crusader he strode over to Vallert, who was bent over in agony. "I warned you that it was dangerous to annoy Miss Savile, Vallert. It is no less so to annoy me, and I should take it amiss if you continued in London during Miss Savile's stay here. In fact . . ."

"That's enough, Alma," Diana cried. "Lord Vallert will not bother me again."

Alma glanced at her determined countenance, and then merely said to Vallert, "I hope you understand me."

Vallert made no reply but nodded and Alma mounted Crusader, his face grimly set. When they were out of earshot he turned to Diana and growled, "What were you about—sending your groom from you? Were you trying to encourage Vallert's advances?"

"No more than I tried to encourage yours, Alma," she snapped at him.

His face flushed and he murmured, "I should never have forced myself on you."

"No, there was no need, was there?" she whispered, stricken.

"You know I didn't mean that, Diana," he said softly. "I was alarmed at having hurt you, and you were shaken. Please do not dwell on it."

"Of course not," she replied stoutly. "Vallert asked if I would send my groom to tell his friend which direction we had taken."

"You might have known he had no friend coming," he said exasperatedly.

"The thought did occur to me, Alma, but I had

rather have faith in a man's honorable behavior than view everyone with suspicion. I will be more distrustful in future."

"London is not like the country where you know everyone, Diana. You could get yourself in serious trouble by being too trusting."

"Yes, my lord."

"I don't mean to scold you. I am only concerned for your welfare."

"That is kind of you."

"You need not be pert with me, miss. What would your brother say to such an episode?"

"What did he say to you?"

"We're not discussing me!" Alma roared.

"I do not want you to tell George," she said softly.

"He must be told, Diana. What if I had not come along when I did?"

She gazed at him incredulously. "You cannot be serious. What did you have to do with it? I was perfectly capable of handling the situation, as you saw for yourself."

Alma had the grace to flush, but said stubbornly, "Yes, I admit that you managed to extract yourself *this* time, Diana, but you should not allow yourself to think that it would always be so."

"Yes, I know," she replied sadly. "George taught me what to do, but I do not suppose it would always work."

"Well, it would always work," Alma admitted dryly, "if you had the opportunity. You might well not."

Diana did not reply for a moment. "I think I shall go home."

"Yes, I am taking you there."

"No, I mean to the Park. London is not so amusing after all."

"You must not let one incident upset you, Diana."

"I am not upset."

"Then why should you go back to the Park? George will not want to leave London yet."

"I can go alone. I have a lot to do before George is married."

"Such as?"

"The Dower House is in need of refurbishing before I move there. I had only begun when we left."

Alma's startled glance rested on her. "You are moving into the Dower House? Surely George and Miss Sanfield would not want you to do so."

"No, they do not like the idea much, but I am determined to leave them in peace. Would you want your sister around if you were newly married?"

"I don't have a sister."

"I know that, Alma. The question was hypothetical."

"Yes, well, if you were my sister I am sure I would not mind having you around, Diana." Somehow he felt awkward saying this and he kept his eyes straight ahead.

Diana sighed. "It is not as though I will not be there frequently; but I have been mistress there, Alma, and Alonna should have a chance to take over the position without any interference from me."

Alma considered this for a moment. Undoubtedly that was why George had made an effort to marry off Diana before he himself settled down. Not that he wanted the house free for a new mistress, but because he knew that his sister would not feel able to stay on there when he married. "Will you have a companion at the Dower House?"

"Heavens, no. It is but a five minute walk from the main house, Alma. I shall see George and Alonna every day."

"They will live in London a good part of the year, I suppose."

"Yes, I imagine they will, but then George has done so for years and it has been no problem for me."

They rode on in silence and when they reached George's house, Alma dismounted and handed her down. When he followed her up the steps she turned to him anxiously. "Please don't tell George, Alma."

"I must, unless you will promise me that you will."

Diana did not reply. When the door was opened she went directly to the breakfast room, and he sought out her brother, who was still in his bedchamber. "There is something I should tell you, George," he began.

"Not trying to seduce Diana again, surely," George protested mildly.

"I wish you would not treat her so casually, George," Alma objected. "I was to have ridden with her this morning in the park and I found her fighting off Vallert."

"Presumably you were not on time for your ride, Ellis."

"For God's sake, will you take the matter seriously?"

"Does Diana?"

"No. Yes. I'm not sure."

"Tell me about it."

"I gather Vallert was waiting for her when she arrived, and, yes, I was late. He asked her to leave her groom to inform a nonexistent friend in which direction they had ridden. I know her groom, of course, and he told me. When I found them he was trying to . . . caress her and she kneed him."

"I hope you did not call him out, Ellis."

"I had a mind to, but I didn't think Diana would like it."

"I would not have either."

"I told him to leave town for a while, and your sister had already informed him that she did not wish to be in his company again."

George offered Alma a cup of chocolate which was refused. "Diana does not appear to be very lucky in the men who court her," he observed. "I do not really believe that she's careless or encouraging, do you, Ellis?"

Alma met his eyes with some hostility. "Not encouraging, George, but not altogether careful. She should not have sent the groom away."

"She should have been able to rely on Vallert's gentlemanly conduct."

"I should like to know why, when she is as aware as you are what he did to Miss Sanfield."

"True. Still, they were in a public park. Very well, Ellis, I will speak with her."

"I have already spoken to her, George," Alma said exasperatedly. "I simply thought you should know, and I

160

did not think she would tell you. She says she is going home to the Park."

"Perhaps that would be best," George replied blandly.

"But she will be alone there."

"She is often alone there, Ellis, but she is seldom lonely.

"Could you not convince her to forget about moving into the Dower House?"

"No, we have tried, but she is determined upon it."

"I should hate to accuse you of neglecting your sister, George, but perhaps your own affairs are occupying you to her disadvantage," Alma suggested coldly.

"When you think you could do better, Ellis, you let me know," George replied gently. "Don't let me detain you. I dare say you are impatient to be with Fanny."

Alma bowed stiffly and departed.

chapter seventeen

When Alma left Grosvenor Square he was in rather a temper. Of course he should not have rebuked George for his care of his sister, and certainly Diana would consider that she had nothing of which to complain; but Alma did not like the thought of her leaving London. In the country she would no doubt find numerous interests to stimulate her natural curiosity, but all her friends were in town. It did not seem fair that the disagreeable behavior of a man such as Vallert should drive her from the bustle that was London during the season. Perhaps he would call on her later to see if he could change her mind.

Since Fanny was expecting him this morning he went straight to her house. He was shown directly to her bedchamber, where he found her still in bed, a tray with tea and toast on her knees. "Will you join me, Ellis?"

"You haven't enough to feed a bird there," he retorted, aware that he was indeed, exceedingly hungry.

"I was not speaking of my meal," she replied, with a roguish grin.

He lifted the tray from her lap and set it on a table. "Yes, but I shall expect you to feed me later," he grumbled.

"If you would rather have breakfast," she said with lifted brows, "I will ring for something."

Alma seated himself on the edge of the bed and began taking off his boots. "Yes, do that, please," he said absently.

Fanny was startled but did as she was bid while Alma proceeded to remove his clothes and don the dressing gown which was laid out for him. He took a turn about the room before climbing into bed beside her, where he pensively tied and untied the belt of the dressing gown.

A maid entered and Fanny instructed her to have

breakfast sent up for Lord Alma. Then she turned to her companion and said aggrievedly, "You are not yourself this morning, Ellis. Have you a problem?"

"'No," he replied shortly. "Has anyone ever taught you how to disarm a man if he makes improper advances?"

"I have never wanted to," she replied mockingly.

"I am serious, Fanny. I saw a young lady do it this morning."

"*Most* improper education for a genteel young woman. I hope this is not the explanation for your lack of interest, Ellis," she admonished.

"I do not lack interest," he muttered, stung. "I am very hungry, is all."

"Well, I will just go write a letter while you . . ."

"No, you don't." He put his arm about her shoulders when she moved to leave the bed. "It will be some time before my meal arrives. Stay with me and I will pleasure you. I don't do it often enough for you."

"You are become thoughtful in your dotage, Ellis," she scoffed, but her eyes became softly luminous as his hands gently explored her body. He was one of the few men she entertained who made an effort to please her, and lately he had been more concerned with his own appetite, which was apparently insatiable. Now he urged her to tell him exactly what she wished him to do, and he did it with exquisite results for her. He made no demands of his own, but held her gently when she was satisfied.

His meal was brought shortly afterwards and he attacked it with relish as Fanny studied him pensively. She had known him for several years, off and on. He usually came to London for the season and stayed several months. During the rest of the year he made occasional trips there of shorter duration. She knew he enjoyed her company, and her body; knew just as surely that he did not love her, but she did not expect him to. It was hardly necessary, or even desirable in her chosen life, but he was a favorite of hers and she would miss him when he no longer came. She feared that time was approaching, for his equanimity had been shaken, and she had no doubt it was a woman. The archer? Fanny sighed.

Alma smiled down at her and offered her a bite of beef, but she wrinkled her nose distastefully. He cheerfully proceeded to eat it himself, and to remark that her cook understood well what a man needed for breakfast.

"He has considerable experience," she reminded him playfully.

"So I should suppose. Fanny, do you think a properly brought up young woman experiences desire?"

"Some of them do, but most are so carefully guarded in what they read, how they live, and what they are told that they would not understand it if they did experience it."

"Would it seem likely to you that a young woman who had spent several weeks frequently in a man's company under very loose chaperonage would respond to his advances even if she did not like him?"

Fanny laughed. "Who knows, Ellis? I am not a properly brought up young woman."

"You are a woman. Can you respond to someone you don't like?"

"No, and thank heaven I no longer have to. But even proper ladies are fascinated sometimes by a man's obvious desire."

"Yes, I can see that, but if the young woman had several passionate suitors and rejected them, only to allow this man some privileges, what then?"

"Then it could be that she liked the man, or that the situation was especially provocative."

"Oh," Alma replied, disappointed. The situation had been provocative for him, certainly, but he had not fully considered that it might have been for Diana. Frightening her, wounding her where he had, yes, it might have emotionally charged the situation for her. Alma climbed out of bed and began to dress.

Fanny regarded him with astonishment. "Are you leaving, Ellis?" she asked incredulously.

"Yes," he said, preoccupied. "I have a call to make this afternoon."

She glanced at the ormolu clock on the mantelshelf. "But it is only eleven, Ellis."

"Is it? No matter, I have some errands to run as well."

Casting her eyes heavenward, Fanny asked lightly, "Will I see you later?"

He smiled at her then and said, "Of course, if you are willing."

"Come when you wish, Ellis," she replied resignedly. Under her breath she murmured, "But I hope you will *be here* the next time."

Alma blew her a kiss and strolled out. He stopped at a tobacconist's for snuff, at a goldsmith's for a locket for a cousin's birthday, at a printseller's to survey the latest cartoons, and at White's to see who was there. He then went round to Grosvenor Square and diffidently asked if Miss Savile was at home.

Diana received him in the yellow drawing room where she was alone and playing the song she had taught him. "Now you have made me receive a scold from George, Alma," she teased him as she offered her hand.

He shook it and retorted, "He did not seem the least bit interested. I wonder he bothered."

Her face creased with concern. "Are you angry with George?"

"No, of course not. He must protect you as he sees fit."

"George is a perfect brother," she championed him hotly. "He does not interfere in my life except when necessary, and he treats me just as I would wish."

"He leaves you alone at the Park a great deal of the time."

"I don't care! He has offered me a companion and I will not have one!"

"Let us not argue about it, Diana. If you are satisfied, there is no more to be said."

"Very well," she allowed, the anger dying gradually.

"I trust you are no worse for this morning's adventure?"

A gleam appeared in her eyes. "I have written a new verse, Alma. Would you like to read it?"

"Certainly."

Diana went to the delicate mahogany sheveret and pulled open a drawer. She extracted a sheet of paper, grinned at it in amusement and returned to him. "I call it *London Ways.*" Her eyes were dancing.

Alma took it from her suspiciously and glanced at the neat copperplate:

> *Is virtue here*
> *A single tear*
> *When reputations soil?*
>
> *A chaperone;*
> *No hour alone*
> *Will save her from this coil.*
>
> *Throughout the day*
> *She cannot stray*
> *From guardians fierce and loyal.*
>
> *But every night*
> *A horrid plight*
> *Persistent swains to foil.*

"That's the worst poetry I ever read!" he exclaimed.

"Well, you have not yet finished it, Alma. You must turn it over for the completion." She was laughing now.

> *Address they use*
> *(More like abuse)*
> *To bring passion to the roil.*
>
> *Is it to wed*
> *Or merely bed*
> *This gallantry so royal?*
>
> *She a store*
> *Of sweetness pure*
> *He a drudge to toil.*
>
> *'Tis his mistake*
> *If her he'd take:*
> *She'd boil him well in oil!*

"It is wretched, and highly improper," he accused her, a smile lurking at the corners of his mouth.

"It is not so easy to find words that end in oil," she defended herself. "I was rather pleased with it myself."

"Then you must lack all taste in poetry."

"Yes, another area in which I am sadly remiss. I shall have to study it. Have you some books to recommend to me?"

"Several," he replied dampeningly. "I take it this means you are not overset and may reconsider your decision to return to the Park."

"No, I am ready to go home. I will have to return here several weeks before the wedding in any case, and that will be sufficient time in London for me."

"You won't mind being alone at the Park when all your friends are here?"

"No, how should I? There is the Dower House to work on . . . and my Christmas play," she said, grinning.

"I hope you do not intend to write it in verse."

She laughed. "Oh, Alma, I shall miss you. There is no one like you for dampening my pretentions."

He was strongly tempted to hug her, but he had no intention of attempting another explanation to her brother. "I shall see you on your return, Diana," he said gruffly. "Does George send you in his carriage?"

"He says he will go with me, though I told him there was no need. He thought to take a few days setting everything to rights for bringing Alonna home."

"Tell George I have Crusader matched against Chanticleer Wednesday week if he should care to come over to Newmarket from the Park. I shall be staying there for a few days."

"Could not I come as well?"

Alma flushed slightly. "Certainly, if it would interest you. Barrymore intends to ride his own horse, but I would rather have a jockey on Crusader."

"Is it a costly match?"

"Four hundred guineas." Alma smoothed out a wrinkle in his coat sleeve.

Diana's eyes widened in surprise. "Is that customary?"

"With Barrymore it is minimum, I assure you. He had rather it had been five hundred, but I would not go so high in spite of my confidence in Crusader." Alma unconsciously slipped her verse into his pocket, and she did not notice. "When do you leave for the Park?"

"In the morning."

"I will take leave of you now then. Have a pleasant journey." He took her hand and kissed it lightly.

When Alma left, Diana sat down at the harpsichord once more and played for an hour. Before leaving the room she looked about for the poem but was not disturbed when she did not find it. After all, it had been a joke for Alma and he had read it, so there was no further use for it. Alma came upon it when he was at Fanny's and left it in his pocket since he was far too occupied at the time to think of returning it. Later he reread it with a grin and placed it in his desk, at the same time hoping that Diana would not accompany her brother if he came to Newmarket, as Alma intended to take Fanny with him when he went.

Diana and George arrived at the Park the next evening and discussed the refurbishing of Alonna's suite of rooms. He tried once again to convince Diana to stay in the house rather than move into the Dower House but was unsuccessful. For a few days he occupied himself with matters at the Park, spending a good deal of time riding and fencing with Diana. Although Diana had told him of Alma's projected race, George was eager to return to London and did not stay long enough at the Park to attend.

Work on the Dower House was proceeding well and Diana took time from supervising it to enjoy herself, but she felt an unusual lack of interest in her customary activities. Several days after George's departure she was on her archery range when she heard hoofbeats. She unnocked her arrow, since she had no desire for a repeat of her prior performance. The rider approaching her had his back to the late afternoon sun and she could not see his face, but she felt a certain excitement mount in her when she thought that perhaps Alma had decided to stop by the Park on his return from Newmarket.

The rider called her name as he came closer and she could begin to see him better. "H—Harry?" she stuttered.

"Yes," he replied as he dismounted and strode to where she stood frozen. "I hope I see you well?"

"Very, thank you. And you?"

He made no attempt to take her hand, which she hesitantly offered. "No, I must speak with you first, Diana."

"Let me put away my equipment and we can sit in the garden," she suggested nervously. He took the bow and arrows from her and put them in the shed before following her to the stables. He was dressed in the uniform of the 10th Light Dragoons, a captain.

When he had left his horse with Josh, and Rogue had been freed, they seated themselves on a stone bench in the garden and he studied her carefully. "You look very little older than you did five years ago."

"It is because I am small," she replied inanely.

"Diana, I have no right to ask your forgiveness for what happened that day. For a long time afterwards I was so caught up in my hatred for your brother, the way he treated me, that I was not able to see what I had done. My father bought me a commission in the army shortly thereafter and, well, I have grown up a lot since then, I hope. I can never express to you how deeply sorry I am for my behavior."

The embarrassment that Diana had felt on seeing him again had begun to diminish. "It is long forgotten, Harry. You must not continue to chastise yourself."

He moved restlessly on the bench, his hands brought up to run through his straight blond hair. "I have read my aunt's letters these five years with more than ordinary interest. When time went by and you did not marry, a beautiful young woman such as yourself, I began to fear that I had damaged your reputation beyond repair."

"No such thing! No one but George ever knew of that day, I assure you." She spoke firmly in an effort to erase the torment from his intent gray eyes.

"You relieve my mind," he sighed. "I would like to speak with your brother, if I might, to offer him the apology that is due him."

"George is not at home right now. He is in London with his fiancée, but there is no need to speak with him. Even at the time he took your age into account, as I recall," she said softly. "Are you staying with Mrs. Lewis?"

"Yes, for a short time. She told me she had stayed with you at the Park recently for several weeks."

"Yes, a friend of George's was here, and I had to have a chaperone. Now that is one thing I do hold against you, Harry," she laughed. "I had to have a chaperone for three years after that incident."

He regarded her gravely and retorted, "You would have had one in any case, I believe. If memory serves, your brother had gone to London to scout one out for you."

"Your memory is too faithful," she admitted. "Will you have tea with me?"

"I do not think I should."

Her eyes danced with amusement. "Can you still not be trusted?"

Harry responded with a crooked grin. "Certainly I can, Miss Savile, but your brother might not approve."

"I am three-and-twenty now, and in charge of my own life. George is to be married shortly, and I shall live in the Dower House."

"Have you no wish to marry?" he asked gently.

Diana's face clouded momentarily, and she replied after a while, "I really cannot say."

"Surely you have suitors," he prodded.

"Oh, yes, several of them, but I cannot seem to like any one of them well enough to marry him," she remarked sadly.

Harry followed her into the small parlor where she rang for tea. It occurred to him that perhaps she felt that she had given him her heart those many years ago, as she had very nearly given him her body, and that she was unable to do so again.

Diana broke into his revery. "Have you wed, Harry?"

"No, a soldier's life is not much to offer a woman. I am being considered for a post in the Foreign Office now, however, and may begin to lead a more settled life if I am offered it."

"Would you like such a post?" she asked curiously.

"Very much. My older brother is there and he enjoys his work."

They discussed the events in their lives since last they met, and Diana found him grown into a serious, level-headed man with easy address and polished manners. When he suggested that they might ride together the next day, she easily accepted with no fear of ungentlemanly conduct.

Diana thought it wisest to write to her brother and inform him of Harry's arrival in the neighborhood, and to assure him of the rectitude of her former would-be lover. At the same time she wrote Alma, thanking him for the poetry books he had sent and confiding that she was not, after all, without companionship in the country.

Then she shrugged off the feeling of loneliness which had begun to creep over her of late, much to her confusion, and devoted herself to her work on the Dower House and her daily rides and drives with Harry. She introduced him to the chariot and he found it a challenge. He was more than a little amused by her explanation of its coming into being, for she grew to feel comfortable enough with him to explain the archery accident, if not the surgery.

It did not escape Harry's notice that she spoke of Alma frequently, what they had done together, how she had tried to amuse him. He sensed the ambivalence of her feelings; and, as he came to know her again, he wondered if he were wise to remain in Linton. Harry was finding that the enchanting girl of eighteen had become a woman of uncommon beauty and delightful fascination.

chapter eighteen

"I cannot like it, Alonna," George confessed to his fiancée when he arrived at her father's home after receiving the letter from Diana. "I do not doubt that Harry Lewis is become a respectable young man in the years since I met him, if Diana says he has. She is not often faulty in her judgment of people."

Alonna looked up from the letter he had given her to read. "Then what troubles you, George?"

"When Diana met this fellow some five years ago she fell in love with him and very nearly damaged her reputation irretrievably." He did not wish to go into the details of the scene he had come upon, even with the woman he loved, but he wanted her to see the situation as he did. "I was very rough on the young man and ordered him away from her. Lord, Alonna, she was young, but old enough to know better."

"She had no mother's guidance, George."

"I know, and her governess, Miss Parston, had recently left her, so that she was at the time without anyone to lay a restraining hand on her. When I arrived I was very heavy-handed about the matter. I forbade Diana to see him again, which I really had to do; but do you not see that the very nature of their parting left her suspended? She had no time to bid him farewell, no chance to hear from him that he regretted his behavior, if indeed he did."

"Yes, I can see that would be very unsatisfactory."

"And now he arrives penitent, a handsome young man who is matured into a worthy fellow. It is not that I fear he will seduce her, but that she will mistake her own feelings for him, having been thwarted so long ago. I really should go to the Park. She is alone there."

"But, George, our engagement ball is tomorrow night," Alonna said wistfully.

"Yes, love, I know, and that is why I am chafing so

I cannot go to her, and I cannot without reason order her to town."

They were interrupted at this point by the butler announcing Lord Alma, who was following at his heels and entered before Alonna had a chance to agree to have him admitted. Alma was waving a letter and appeared disturbed.

"George, have you heard from your sister?" he demanded.

"Yes, this morning."

"So have I, and I do not like the sound of it," he asserted.

"Whatever is my sister doing writing to you?" George asked mildly.

"I sent her some books and she wrote to thank me."

"I cannot see anything in that to upset you."

Alma regarded him belligerently. "You are deliberately misunderstanding me, George."

"Yes," George sighed. "You are disturbed because she mentioned an old acquaintance arrived in the neighborhood, are you not?"

"Are not you?" he shot back.

"Somewhat," George temporized. "Diana writes that Mr. Lewis has become a perfectly respectable young man."

"She is there alone, George."

"I am aware of it."

"Well, are you going to go to her?"

"You forget that my engagement ball is tomorrow night, Ellis. I cannot go."

"Then you must have her come to you," Alma retorted stubbornly, his black brows drawn thunderously ow.

"I cannot think Diana would like that."

"Are you going to do nothing?" Alma asked coldly.

"I cannot see that it is any concern of yours, Ellis, but if it will relieve your mind I intend to go to the Park the day after the ball."

"Her virtue must wait on your pleasure, of course," Alma said sardonically.

"Understand this, Ellis, I am not concerned for her virtue. Diana is quite capable of maintaining it herself, as you well know."

Alma flushed and cast a glance at Alonna, who had sat silently through the whole exchange. He attempted to keep his voice calm as he said, "I beg to differ with you. Have you not considered that it was this same young man who introduced her to . . ." He rubbed a distracted hand over his face. "Lord, George, she is the most curious little thing, and there is something very intriguing about a first love."

"I know," George replied patiently. "That is why I will go in a few days, but I do not think you need to worry about Diana, Ellis. She is very sensible."

Alma nodded, unconvinced. It was not George who had held that passionate little bundle of flesh in his arms. Alma could not bear to think of her in another man's embrace. He rose to take his leave. "Forgive me for barging in on you. I will see you both tomorrow night, no doubt."

When he had left, Alonna turned to George with a smile. "I didn't know he was in love with her."

"He does not know it yet himself," George sighed, "though he is beginning to understand, I think."

"And Diana? Does she love him?"

"Yes, I believe so, but she is almost as bad. They had such a difficult time while he was injured that they find it hard to acknowledge the truth of it."

"They would do well together."

"Yes, if they ever get it sorted out," George grumbled.

Alma went directly to his house and ordered his travelling carriage. He wrote a note to Fanny while his valet packed for him. If George would not do something about the situation, Alma had no intention of letting matters rest. There was an inn in Linton where he could stay, since it would be impossible to stay at the Park. He could be there that very evening.

In actuality it did not turn out to be so simple. First there was the problem of the off leader going lame and

174

very slow journey to the next posting inn in Woodford Wells. Then near Loughton an overturned cart across the road delayed Alma almost an hour. He had a meal at the Black Lion in Bishop's Stortford, was stopped by an inefficient and unsuccessful highwayman short of Quendon and eventually gave up and spent the night at The Horns in Newport, leaving instructions to be called early.

In the morning things went more smoothly and he arrived at the Park at a reasonable hour, an innate caution making him bypass the archery range on his way to the stables. Jenkins was more than a little surprised to see him but made no comment, merely indicating that he believed Miss Diana was in the garden with Mr. Lewis, who had just arrived. When Alma rounded the house and came upon them he stopped dead.

Harry had just burst upon Diana where she was reading poetry on the stone bench and announced that he had been appointed to the post in the Foreign Office. She was delighted for him and thought nothing of it when he jubilantly swung her in a circle and hugged her. "I am so happy for you," she beamed, as she allowed him to continue the grasp he had taken on her hands.

"It is especially important to me because I . . ."

"Diana," Alma said grimly from his spot at the corner of the house.

Her eyes darted to him at the sound of his voice. "Good God, Alma, what are you doing here?"

Although it should have occurred to Alma that he would have to answer this particular question when he arrived, it had not. Instead of answering her he said indignantly, "Obviously it is a good thing that I have come."

"A good thing for whom?" she retorted, the color mounting in her cheeks. Harry released her hands.

Alma had progressed until he stood before them. "George could not come until tomorrow because of his engagement ball."

"There is no need for George to come at all!" she protested. "What is the matter with the two of you? Harry, this is Lord Alma, a friend of my brother's. Alma,

Harry Lewis." The two men bowed stiffly, and Diana continued coldly, "You have not answered my question, Alma."

"I shall discuss it with you in private, Diana."

"Then you may wait in the house. I was speaking with Mr. Lewis when you interrupted us." Her eyes flashed angrily at him, and he glared at her in return.

Harry began gravely, "I assure you, Lord Alma, that there was no impropriety in . . ."

"There is no need for you to explain to him, Harry. It is none of his concern," Diana asserted hotly.

The three stood eyeing each other uncertainly. Diana was the first to regain her composure. "If you will wait for me inside, Alma, I shall be with you in a few minutes. Please."

"Very well." He turned his back on them and disappeared around the side of the house.

"I am sorry for that, Harry. Alma seems to have appointed himself my guardian recently. I doubt George sent him."

"But your brother did obviously find the news of my arrival disturbing enough that he intends to come home," he said sadly. "Not that I blame him, Diana. I behaved reprehensibly when we knew each other years ago, and he is not likely to forget that."

"I told him in my letter that you were become quite respectable," Diana replied with a tremulous smile.

"You cannot expect a loving brother to accept that until he has seen for himself. I started to say a while ago that I was especially pleased about the appointment because it will make my life more settled. Would you consider the possibility of becoming my wife, Diana?"

She regarded him soberly. "You hardly know me, Harry. Or I you. You must not let our experience in the past lead you to such a rash gesture."

He shook his head emphatically. "That has little to do with it, I promise you, Diana. I have enjoyed the time we have spent together these last few days more than I can tell you."

"I have enjoyed it, too, Harry, but I cannot believe it is enough on which to base a decision of marriage."

"I only ask you to consider the possibility, Diana. I must go to London directly, and I cannot say when I will be able to return."

She smiled at him. "I will be in London in about a month. Perhaps I shall see you there."

"You can be sure of it," he grinned. "I shall say good-bye now, but I shall seek your brother out in London so that he will not make a journey to no purpose." His mouth twisted mournfully.

"George is not one to hold a grudge, Harry, but I would appreciate your preventing him from dashing about on my behalf." She extended her hand and he lifted it to his lips and kissed it lightly.

When he had disappeared from sight Diana sighed and wearily made her way to the small parlor where Alma awaited her. She did not relish the thought of their interview. He rose when she entered and she waved him back into his seat while she sat down.

"Does George know you're here, Alma?"

"No."

"Then I would greatly appreciate your explaining to me why you are."

Alma did not look at her, but out the window, while he spoke. "I had your letter and I remembered George mentioning Mr. Lewis, so I went to George and . . ."

"Yes?" she prompted him.

"He could see that it would be wise for him to come to the Park, but he has the engagement ball this evening and could not come until tomorrow."

"Do not tell me you thought he would approve of your coming in his stead," she said scathingly.

"Well, no, I am sure he would not, but I could not leave you alone with such a man around."

"I told you in my letter, Alma, that he is become a perfectly acceptable man, did I not?"

"Yes."

"And you could not believe me?"

"It was not that. There are tons of plausible rascals, Diana."

"Yes, I seem to have met a number of them. You men live by your own rules, I notice, and expect women

177

to live by a different set which you have established for us."

Alma restlessly rose from his chair and paced about the room, eventually stopping in front of her. He spoke gently. "Listen to me, Diana. I came here because I did not want you to be seduced by that man. You have every reason to censure me for my behavior the day we fenced, but you must remember that you responded to me. I am aware that you had sufficient control to stop us; I cannot believe that I would have taken your virtue, but there is no reason for you to believe that if you do not wish to. It was *because* of that experience that I came. George felt it was our proximity which created it, and it seemed to me that the same thing could happen with Lewis. More so with Lewis than anyone else, perhaps, since you had been fond of him before. You might have been right that he had changed, but I could not take that chance."

Silent tears streamed down Diana's cheeks and Alma handed her his handkerchief. "If I was wrong, I am sorry. When I came upon you and he was hugging you, I thought I was right. If I embarrassed you, I did not mean to." Her tears continued to flow, and much as he wanted to comfort her, he would not touch her. He walked over to the window where he stood facing out. After a while he said, "If you can assure me that there is no danger to you, I shall leave now."

Diana gulped back a sob and said, "He brought good news of a post he has obtained in the Foreign Office. He was not making an improper advance, nor has he since he arrived."

Alma turned and came over to her. "Shall I tell George not to bother to come?"

"Harry was leaving immediately for London and said he would see George so that he need not make the trip."

Alma paled slightly at her words. "Is there an understanding between you and Mr. Lewis, Diana?"

She regarded him perplexedly. "An understanding? Oh, you mean of marriage. No, Alma, we have merely agreed to see each other in London when I return there."

"I see. Have I sunk myself irretrievably with you, or may I see you in London, too?" he asked awkwardly.

"Of course you may see me." She dropped her eyes to her clasped hands. "I was upset that you and George should distrust me, but I am grateful that you were concerned enough to come to me in case I needed help."

"I will always be there if you need me, Diana." He stood staring at her downturned head, very conscious of what he had just said and that he meant it. What he wanted was to do just that, to marry her and take care of her, to cherish this inquisitive, charming woman always. But even more than that he wanted her to be happy, and he had seldom made her happy for long. She should have time to decide whether Lewis would make her happy; and hopefully she would grant Alma the opportunity to show that he could do so, if indeed he could.

He cleared his throat and she looked up at him, her eyes red and her cheeks tear-stained. "If I am to put in an appearance at Miss Sanfield's ball I must leave now. Are you all right?"

"Y—yes. T—tell George he has no need for concern." She dried the last of the tears and smiled pathetically at him. "This morning I was reading the poetry books you sent; it was thoughtful of you."

"There is a very fine library at Stillings, as well as at my house in London. When your curosity is aroused on some subject you have only to let me know and I will see what I have."

"I don't suppose you know anything about water distribution in London, do you?" she asked wistfully.

He regarded her perplexedly, and then shrugged his shoulders. "No, my dear, but I will see what I can find before you return to London." His face broadened into a smile as he realized where this particular interest had arisen, and he was grateful that she had come to him for information.

"Did Crusader win his match?"

"Yes, but it was a very near thing, and I do not intend to race him again." He picked up his elegant beaver and turned it in his hands. "Good-bye, Diana. I

179

look forward to seeing you in town." He took her hand in a firm clasp.

"Good-bye, Alma. Thank you for coming." Diana sadly watched him leave and then went into the music room and sat down at the harpsichord. Her fingers wandered over the keys and for the first time in her life the melody she devised was melancholy. She felt hurt that Alma would consider her capable of improper behavior with Harry, but then she supposed George had told him of her previous experience, and she herself had behaved incredibly loosely with Alma. The memory of that morning brought a flush to her cheeks, but more of desire than embarrassment. She did not experience that feeling any longer with Harry, though she enjoyed his companionship. Suddenly she thought about the future, after George and Alonna were wed. She would live in the Dower House, alone. Of course every day, when they were at the Park, she would see George and Alonna, probably often see Allison and Walter, but she might never see Alma again since she did not go often to London.

Diana thought of him then in a way she had never thought of him before, the disparate elements of their relationship coming together in her mind. He was no longer simply the attractive friend of her brother's to be entertained, nor the sulky young man embarrassed by her callous treatment of his body when she removed the arrow. Nor was he the grateful companion presented with the chariot, or the antagonist in their battle of wills. He was also the friend who came to her rescue, and the only person she had found peace with. In his presence sometimes, as on their fishing expeditions, she had been content just to be with him; no plans for future projects distracted her from that enjoyment.

And there was the physical attraction she felt for him, that she did not feel for Harry or Walter or Frank or Vallert. There was the envy she felt of Fanny who did not have to repulse his advances, but could welcome him to her whenever she wished.

Diana stared sightlessly out the windows, her hands unmoving on the keyboard. For the first time she accepted the fact that she loved Alma, that she was lonely when she was not with him, that their encounters made her feel alive as nothing else could. She understood that her desire was based on that love, just as years ago her desire of Harry had been based on the youthful love she had had for him.

Did Alma care for her? He had cared enough to come to her today, but she could not be sure how deep that concern ran. I will always be there if you need me he had said. But would he be there if she needed him always?

Diana rose from the harpsichord, straightened the ornaments on the mantelpiece and went in to luncheon. She had a month before she returned to London and there was much to be done at the Park.

chapter nineteen

George was agreeably surprised by Harry Lewis, who arrived and begged an interview with him minutes before he was due to leave for the ball. The fact that Harry was in town relieved George's mind and he asked the younger man to accompany him in his carriage so that he would not arrive late. Harry agreed and, when the carriage had started, said, "I appreciate your allowing me to speak with you, Mr. Savile. I have a great deal to apologize for which I fear you can never forgive. Perhaps it will help you to know that I came years ago to understand how reprehensible my behavior was and have agonized over the memory of it."

"You could not have believed it proper at the time," George commented dryly.

"No, but I honestly do not think I understood the gravity of it as I might have. I was intoxicated by Diana and used to having what I wanted." He sighed. "I know there is no excuse, but I beg you will believe me that there is no danger to your sister in my company now."

"I will be happy to believe that. In any case I believe you would find Diana more prudent now. Do you return to Linton?"

"No," Harry replied. "I have just received a position in the Foreign Office. I hope, with your permission, to see Diana when she returns to town though."

George studied the young man for a moment. "I have no objection, Mr. Lewis, but I might warn you that I feel her affections are already engaged."

Harry nodded thoughtfully. "She did not say anything, but she spoke of someone frequently." He decided to allow Alma to explain for himself his visit to the Park.

The carriage stopped before Lord Franston's house and George shook hands with Harry. Before stepping down he wished the young man well in his new post, and then directed the coachman to take Harry where he wished. Harry regretfully watched him disappear into the house. Things might have been very different if he had not been such a fool five years ago; he had no one but himself to blame. Diana's brother was remarkably polite considering the circumstances of their previous meeting. He instructed the coachman to take him to his lodgings.

George and Alonna were fully occupied for the next few hours greeting guests and leading the dancing, but George was puzzled that Alma had not arrived. When he finally put in an appearance late in the evening he looked tired and distracted, but he endeavored to enter into the spirit of the evening nonetheless. After many of the guests had departed he approached George and asked if he might have a word with him.

"I must stay until the bitter end, Ellis," George grinned.

"May I await you at your house?"

"Could we not speak in the morning?"

"I would rather not."

"Very well. It may be a while, though," George replied wryly.

Alma nodded and made his farewells to Lord Franston and Alonna before ordering his carriage. Standing in the hall with the buzz of voices sounding faintly from the ballroom, he wondered if he had finally done something which would stretch George's friendship too far. Alma valued that friendship highly and felt depressed at the thought of losing it, but he shrugged off his moodiness when he entered the carriage and allowed himself to think of George's sister.

Once Alma had convinced George's skeptical servants that George had indeed expected him to await his arrival, the hours stretched slowly toward dawn. Alma had fallen asleep in a comfortable leather armchair in the library and George was hesitant to awaken him, but he removed the book from his lap and rang for brandy and glasses. When these were set down and the servants dismissed for the night, he poured two glasses and gently shook Alma's shoulder.

Puzzled eyes gazed up at him before Alma remembered where he was. He straightened up in his chair and said, "Sorry. I didn't mean to fall asleep."

George surveyed him with amusement. "It is practically morning, Ellis. Why don't you use a guest room and we will talk later?"

"No." Alma blinked a few times and took a sip from the glass George offered him. "Have you talked with Lewis?"

George was in the process of replacing his glass on a table and turned startled eyes to his friend. "Yes. How did you know he was in town?"

Alma rubbed his face. "I was at the Park this morning, George."

His friend's lips tightened. "I told you I would go tomorrow."

"I know." Alma frowned. "I knew you would not approve of my going, so I did not tell you."

"I find it ironic, Ellis, that you should take it upon yourself to guard Diana's virtue," George said cuttingly.

"Of course you do," Alma retorted. "If I had thought of it, I probably would have, too, but I only thought that I could not allow any harm to come to her. I love her, George."

A slow smile spread over George's face. "It is about time you came to realize it, Ellis."

Alma responded with a faint grin before his countenance became serious. "She was in no danger, George. I daresay Lewis is not such a bad fellow."

"No, he seemed sincere in his reform."

"I could not tell how she felt about him. She has agreed to meet him when she comes to London." Alma took another sip of his brandy.

"You did not speak to her then?" George asked exasperatedly.

"I want her to be happy, George, and it may be that she was renewed an attachment to him. She should have a chance to decide."

"How is she to decide if she does not know how you feel?"

"I shall tell her when she comes to London. You

184

would not object?" Alma asked seriously. Then he said with a crooked grin, "I believe I meet all your specifications."

"Yes," George agreed, "I believe you do. We will let her decide. Will you go home now, Ellis? I am exhausted."

Alma did not rise until past noon the next day, and he sent a note to Fanny before he went down to his breakfast. She suggested that he call at three, and he presented himself at the appointed hour, feeling slightly foolish but determined. Fanny's own sixth sense had alerted her to dress discreetly and welcome him in the parlor.

"It was thoughtful of you to let me know that you would be out of town, Ellis. I hope you had a pleasant trip." She offered him her hand, which he shook. Her suspicions confirmed, she seated herself in a chair rather than on the sofa and waved him to another.

"I . . . yes, I suppose it was in some ways. Certainly it was important. Fanny, I have decided to marry a young woman if she will have me; and I think it would be best if I did not see you any more." He brushed a crease out of his elegant pantaloons.

"You think she would object?" Fanny asked curiously.

"Not that so much as that she would probably think it unfair," Alma admitted.

"Unfair?"

"That I could do as I please when she cannot," he explained.

Fanny laughed appreciatively. "I think I would like her."

"Yes, I feel sure you would, and she would probably like you but . . ." He stopped, confused.

"But it is not likely we will meet, Ellis," she said gently.

"No." He sat there silent for a while before he said, "I wonder, Fanny, if I might ask you . . . how best to . . . well, when a woman has not been with a man before . . . it must be . . . somewhat frightening."

"Of all men I know, Ellis, I would best trust you with a virgin," Fanny replied. "But I will tell you what I can."

When Alma left he gave her a handsome present, thanked her for her frankness with him and kissed her warmly. Fanny wished him well and found it necessary to visit her favorite modiste to choose a new gown to cheer her.

On an exceedingly hot day at the beginning of June, Diana arrived in London. She had completed the renovation of the Dower House to her satisfaction and seen that George's instructions for Alonna's suite were carried out. Although these projects had not unduly strained her endurance, George was concerned when he saw her, for her usual glow was somewhat lacking. She professed to excellent health, however, and he did not pursue the matter. Both Alma and Harry called on the day after her arrival, at precisely the same time. They were civil to one another and exceedingly gallant to Diana, but she felt suddenly nervous in Alma's presence and the visit was rather awkward. She was not loath to see them depart together.

For several days she was kept busy attending to her wardrobe for George's wedding, and assisting Alonna with her preparations. She was seldom at home and each day found cards from Alma and usually from Harry. Finally George took matters in hand and invited Alma to dine with him a week after Diana's arrival. His sister and Alonna were the only other members of the party.

Alma arrived before George returned with his fiancée and he seated himself beside Diana on a sofa. "I have been sorry to miss you so often, Diana."

"Yes, it has been a busy week."

"I imagine things are fairly well organized for the wedding now," he said hopefully.

"Yes, I plan to take some time for myself these next few days," she offered encouragingly.

"Perhaps we could ride together in the morning."

"I would like that."

George and Alonna entered to interrupt their mundane conversation and discussion became general for the next two hours. When they had sung several pieces together George announced that he wished to ask Alonna's advice on redecorating the breakfast parlor, and the two of them departed.

Diana had remained at the harpsichord and in her nervousness picked out the melancholy air she had composed at the Park. When Alma said he did not believe he knew the song she replied, "It is one of mine."

"I thought you only composed happy songs, Diana."

"Usually I do."

"Will you come and sit with me?"

She nodded but found it difficult to rise from the bench. He smiled encouragingly at her and held out his hand where he stood above her. She allowed him to draw her to her feet and immediately released her grip. The sofa was not long, but she managed to sit as far from him as possible.

"Diana, I know we have not always had an easy time together," he began, his intent eyes holding hers, "and I know that it has usually been my fault. I can think of no reason why you should return my regard; I can merely hope that you do. I have only recently realized that I love you and that I want more than anything to marry you." He watched her countenance soften from the anxious look it had worn. "If you find that seeing Mr. Lewis again has revived the emotions you felt for him once, I can understand. Or if you do not care for me, of course." He paused but she did not speak, so he hastened on. "Perhaps you would like some time to get to know Mr. Lewis again, but I would like a chance to show you that I am not always short-tempered and surly, too."

Diana gave a gurgle of laughter and stretched out her hand to him. He took it firmly, his eyes questioning. "Oh, Alma, it is no wonder I did not realize I loved you, when I think of those weeks you spent at the Park. I should have known, though, when you kissed me," she said shyly.

"Yes, and so should I. When you suggested that we

bet on the outcome of the chariot race the first thing that came to my mind was to wager you a kiss, and I could not understand where the idea came from."

"Alma?"

"Yes, love?"

"Will you . . . continue to see that pretty girl?"

"No, Diana. I have not seen her for a month now, since I decided I wanted to marry you."

"Really?" Her eyes sparkled. "I would never have asked it of you. George explained to me how it is with men."

"That was thoughtful of him," Alma drawled, "and highly improper."

"Oh, he did not explain it recently," Diana hastened to add.

His hand which still held hers drew her to him. "If you will recall that George and Alonna are but a few doors away, I will kiss you," he mocked her.

"I am pleased that you reminded me, Alma," she replied pertly as she surrendered to his embrace. The fire which had touched her before recurred and she drew away breathlessly. "I do not think we should be alone much before we're married," she said with a grin.

"I'm sure sufficient of your time will be consumed in studying the materials I have gathered for you on water distribution in London that you will have little enough time for me," he retorted. "I assure you that I am perfectly trustworthy," he continued staidly, but his eyes gleamed in the candlelight and he pulled her into his arms again.

When George and Alonna returned to the room they regarded the embracing couple complacently. George turned to Alonna and murmured, "I think they have finally sorted it out. Would you like to see the solarium?"

YOUR WARNER LIBRARY OF REGENCY ROMANCE

THE BEST OF REGENCY ROMANCE
FROM WARNER BOOKS

THE ROMANY REBEL
by Zabrina Faire   (94-206, $1.75)

Lord Roxbrough had taken charge of young Easter Hazel-tyne's life and decreed she was to be presented in town. Together they would rearrange the plans and life of the cold Lord Roxbrough.

ENCHANTING JENNY
by Zabrina Faire   (94-103, $1.75)

Jenny said, "No!" but everyone else insisted that this was the right marriage for Jenny. The Conte was the scion of a noble family and Jenny's sisters' chances for marriage would improve when she became the Contesse. But only Jenny herself was opposed to the match.

THE SEVENTH SUITOR
by Laura Matthews   (94-340, $1.75)

Kate had just refused her fifth marriage proposal for even she had to laugh at the absurd prank her brother's friends were playing. But she remembered that years ago she had refused such a proposal, and there had been sad consequences. Now all she had to remember that suitor by was a legacy that no lady of honor would accept.

THE SMILE OF THE STRANGER
by Joan Aiken   (94-144, $1.75)

She spoke Italian and French with fluency and knew more English history than many a girl born and reared in England. She managed it all until she met the man who looked like her dream hero and begged to be her love.

PULSE-RACING, PASSIONATE, ADVENTURE-FILLED FICTION

CASABLANCA INTRIGUE
by Clarissa Ross   **(91-027, $2.50)**

Morocco, 1890. Beautiful Gale Cormier is on her honeymoon. Her husband is talking to a dark man in a red fez . . . at least, he was a moment ago. Now she is alone as a curious crowd moves in upon her . . . examining . . . begging . . . menacing . . .

CARESS AND CONQUER
by Donna Comeaux Zide   **(82-949, $2.25)**

She was Cat Devlan, a violet-eyed, copper-haired beauty bent on vengeance. She was a living challenge to Ryan Nicholls, but was she the mistress of a pirate as she claimed when they first met? Or the favorite of the King of France? . . . and a Murderess?

LIBERTY TAVERN
by Thomas Fleming   **(91-220, $2.50)**

The American Revolution is love and hate, a beautiful woman, flogged for loving a Royalist. It is a young idealist who murders in the cause of liberty. "A big historical novel with a bracing climate of political sophistication."

                          —*New York Times Book Review*